DOLLS DON'T CHOOSE

Detective Chief Inspector Bob Southwell is not best pleased when his rival, Detective Superintendent Hallam, arrives as his new boss. Bob Southwell is already under pressure to solve a wave of attacks on women in York. When the attacks begin to centre on the university, Southwell has the crazy idea that Hallam may somehow be involved. Or is it so crazy ...? Meanwhile, at the university, blonde student Angela has become involved with the Women's Group and the first murder acts as a focus for all her insecurity, to the point where she is prepared to put herself in a position of real danger ...

DOLLS DON'T CHOOSE

DOLLS DON'T CHOOSE

by

Barbara Whitehead

Magna Large Print Books
Long Preston, North Yorkshire,
England.

British Library Cataloguing in Publication Data.

Whitehead, Barbara
  Dolls don't choose.

  A catalogue record for this book is
  available from the British Library

  ISBN 1-7505-1470-1

First published in Great Britain by Constable & Company
Ltd., 1998

Published in Large Print 2000 by arrangement with Constable
& Company Ltd.

Magna Large Print is an imprint of
Library Magna Books Ltd.
Printed and bound in Great Britain by
T.J. International Ltd., Cornwall, PL28 8RW.

For Alan, Roger and John

1

Detective Chief Inspector Robert Southwell never forgot the minutes he spent waiting in the group of senior police officers standing on the tarmac at Fulford Road Police Headquarters. They were waiting for the new detective superintendent to arrive. It was late summer, in fact early autumn, and the weather was still unreasonably hot. He had been asked to be there because he had been acting detective superintendent himself for months, and the man they were expecting was his new boss. Of course Bob had wanted the post himself. During the waiting, he went over in his mind every stage of the selection process. He'd applied, he'd worked his guts out studying and trying to guess what questions they would ask at the assessments, he'd got as far as the short list and gone down to the residential centre for the two days when the final decision was going to be made. Six of them had been there, going through the tests and interviews, and the only man he'd disliked in the group was now on his way to become the new permanent detective superintendent. The worst of it was that Bob had been told—unofficially—that he had been the runner-up, the second on the list.

The longer they stood there the hotter they felt. Bob could feel his shirt sticking to his back. At least the blighter might have had the decency to arrive on time. There weren't any traffic jams up in the sky, were there?

The helicopter droned into view.

Trust Bruno Hallam to make this sort of a stir. Why couldn't he travel by car like most people? Or the train? That would save the police force some money. But no. Not our Bruno.

The helicopter was not the pleasantest way to travel, Bruno Peter Ralph Hallam thought on the journey from the city of Sheffield. The noise and vibration outweighed the fascination of flying this way. All the same, it was interesting to look down, first on the centre of the big city, then on its far outflung suburbs, not patterned into the landscape like old villages and towns but placed on it with no consideration for contour, the houses all alike, rows of buns in a baker's shop. The old smoky industry had expired painfully some years ago, so he could see every detail clearly below him. This was his native city he was leaving. The twang of its accent was familiar in his ears; he knew the places, including 't'Wicker where t'watter runs o'er t'weir', and could ask 'What's up wi' thee?' with the broadest-accented of his compatriots. But, love the city as he did, it was a long time since he had felt parochial. He had travelled and worked in many places.

They flew nor-nor-east and he could pick out in the distance cooling towers, the flash of rivers, scattered ancient hamlets. The motorways gleamed with cars, vans, artics, great lumbering vehicles of all sorts transporting, as it were, coals to

Newcastle, goods from far away to places where they could have been perfectly well manufactured in the first place.

They moved towards the softer country of the Vale of York, and ahead he saw York Minster, gleaming pale in the sun.

On the ground, the waiting group of police officers was watching the approach of the helicopter. At last, it was overhead. It seemed to descend slowly, circling, the noise loud enough to deafen, the wind from its blades strong enough to make the uniformed men on the tarmac below hold on to their hats. It came to rest with precision, opposite the waiting officers. The blades slowed and stopped.

After what seemed like a long time and was actually a few seconds, the helicopter door opened and they saw a thickset man climb out and walk towards them. He looked calm and cool. Reaching the group, he was greeted by the highest-ranking officer there, and was then introduced to everyone, shaking hands.

After a half a minute the helicopter started its engine up deafeningly and soared off into the sky, taking its other passengers on to Newcastle-upon-Tyne. Its flight had only been interrupted briefly to accommodate Bruno Hallam.

Bruno Hallam was regarded as a white hope, a high-flyer, the best thing since sliced bread. Great things were expected of him. York thought it was privileged to get him, to snatch him from Sheffield. Every few years, applications for such posts had to be open to the whole country, but no one had expected Bruno to apply. Granted it was a grade up, but York was a peaceful place compared to the big conurbations. He was hardly climbing the ladder, coming here.

Except that this summer, during these incredibly hot days, this unusually stifling heat wave, the city had become a place of fear to the women who lived here. A series of assaults had begun and had been going on for long enough to become a threat. Whatever their age, the women of York carried fear with them, and were unable to forget the dark irrational dread. They carried the fear with them as if it were a sucking child. It was equally impossible to put out of mind. Waking or sleeping, it was in their thoughts. So far no one had been killed, but they were all convinced that it was only a matter of time.

Perhaps now Bruno Hallam was here, the menace would end. He would catch the 'rapist'—so the women thought of him, but he was only a would-be rapist, for so far the attacker had not succeeded in what they took to be his aim. And Bob Southwell was sick at heart, because he wanted to catch the attacker himself, and he had liked being detective superintendent, he had liked it very much. Not sufficient experience, his boss had told him. Apply again the next time. It was all rubbish. He'd had plenty of experience. They had just wanted the other chap, that was it.

Bruno was suddenly there in front of him, stretching out his hand, and Bob put his own out in response. They clasped, and Bruno Hallam smiled at him; Bob smiled back, feeling the smile make his face taut in the sunshine.

'Good to see you again, Bob,' Bruno

said in a sincere way. 'You'll be showing me the ropes.'

'With pleasure,' replied Bob. 'See you as soon as this lot's done with you.'

Bruno gave him the suggestion of a wink. You and I, said the wink, we do the real work. We have to humour these stuffed shirts.

They were a physical contrast. Bob was tall and thin, even bony. He wore large spectacles which caught reflections and often made his expression enigmatic. He walked lightly as though he were a dancer, and reminded many people of Fred Astaire. His forehead was broad. He was an intelligent and efficient officer, with that extra something which made him stand out from the crowd. Flair, keenness, fairness—a quality much valued by his men—sharpness, like the sharpness of a blade. He was impatient with slowness and slovenliness, quick to reward good results and give credit where it was due.

Bruno Hallam was shorter and more sturdy. His walk was strong and deter-mined. He did not need glasses and his neck was size seventeen. His fingers were firm and his handclasp not quickly forgotten. After the seconds of comradeship with Bob Southwell, he finished his round of greetings and everyone was left with some moment to remember, some personal word or touch, an impression of strength.

The canteen staff had laid out a cold lunch in a room next to the canteen, so that the little gathering could get to know Hallam in peace for half an hour. Bob ate and chatted to a few colleagues and then began longing to get away. He didn't really like the Fulford nick. Granted it was his headquarters and much newer than Clifford Street, but he preferred Clifford Street and mostly worked there. Every time he tried to catch Hallam's eye it wasn't possible—he was always absorbed in conversation.

At last Bob made his way over, touched Hallam's arm, and said, 'Sorry to interrupt, but I think I'd better be getting back to Clifford Street.'

Hallam turned.

'I hope to be down later, Bob,' he said.

Bob Southwell slid unobtrusively out of the door and was instantly reminded of the reasons he hated this building. The corridors were square and claustrophobic. It was like walking along inside a box, a square box, airless, which went on for ever, with other low-ceilinged boxes opening off it.

With a feeling of relief he reached the open air. Behind him he was sure that lunch would still be in noisy progress an hour hence, for they all seemed to be enjoying themselves. Longing to be away from buildings in general, he crossed the busy road and took his way downhill on a typical suburban avenue towards the river. At the bottom the Ouse, wide and khaki-coloured, slid along a few feet below the tow-path. Bob Southwell turned right and walked towards the centre of York. He was overtaken from time to time by cyclists swishing along. The tow-path was tree-shaded and cooler than the asphalt behind Fulford nick. The houses, standing well back from the river, were old and interesting—and also amongst the most expensive in the city. Strolling there was a release. Several times he stood still and breathed deeply. Elderly women with small dogs walked past him as he stood. By the time he reached New Walk—it had been given that name when it was created, back in the eighteenth century—he was ready to face life again. But he had realised something. He had lost confidence in himself. There was a sinking feeling inside which he had never experienced before, yet here he was, nearly back at his place of work, needing to resume at least the appearance of authority.

Colliergate and Clifford Street meant his place of work to Bob Southwell (pronounced Suthell). He loved the red-brick walls in that area, contrasting with the creamy stone of York Castle which is nearly opposite the Magistrates' Court and police offices. They might be out of date, but they were central and he could reach any part of the ancient city centre on foot in a few minutes, or stalk off, reaching home in quarter of an hour with his long strides. At one time this had been the police headquarters for York, and a lot of police work still took place here. Traffic control was an important part of it. Passing through the busy office on the ground floor, Bob took the stairs two at a time.

'You must be fit,' said Sergeant Diamond, watching him come up. 'In this heat! You must be fit.'

'Not really. Only pleased to get away from Fulford.'

'Oppressive in that building, isn't it?' The older man didn't mind admitting what Bob would never have confessed to.

'I prefer it here,' said Bob, realising that all his staff were gathered together and looking at him like dogs at a bone.

'Won't be a minute,' he said, and walked through them to his office. His own old office, the office of a detective chief inspector. Shutting the door behind him he leaned against it. Dave Smart, on temporary promotion, had occupied this room while Bob was acting detective superintendent. Dave had cleared his stuff out carefully but the place still felt alien to Bob, like an old coat someone else had been wearing, now become a stranger to its owner. He crossed to the window and looked down on tatty, familiar Clifford Street. He knew this street from this window in all seasons, under snow and under sun. His hands clutched the edges of the windowsill to brace his slim body as he leaned forward and pressed his brow to the inner layer of glass, looking down at the passers-by.

The rather grander and more spacious superintendent's office upstairs would soon be occupied by Bruno Hallam.

Bob began to feel he was not being fair to the other staff. He had shut the door on them although he could see they were dying to ask him questions. After a minute's solitude, he realised that he did not know what to do with himself. He felt miserable, alone there in his old place. That problem at least was soon solved. He knew that to his staff he might have seemed churlish, even, God forbid, as though he was sulking.

Southwell opened the door again and

walked back into the outer office, where the whole of the staff were still waiting to talk to him. They wanted to know what the new super was like.

'Bloody hot in here,' said Bob, who swore rarely, 'but it was hotter out there at Fulford waiting on that tarmac.'

'Tell us,' said DI Dave Smart.

Dave was the closest to Bob of all his staff, his friend and a mate as well as a colleague. He stood as tall as Bob but was much more massive, built like a brick wall, with a reddish face and crisply curling black hair. He was showing no sign of regret at returning to his old grade, in fact Bob knew that Dave found it a relief. He had not liked the extra responsibility.

'Well, the helicopter came down and there he was,' Bob said.

'Flashy git,' commented Dave.

Everyone agreed that to make an entrance by helicopter must indicate a high level of flashy git-ness. They were impressed, all the same.

'He's got a bit of panache,' one of the

women detective constables said to DC 'Jenny' (really Gladys) Wren. 'I wonder if he's attractive.'

'Don't know,' said Jenny, who was firmly attached by now to Dave Smart and had stopped considering other men in that light. She had come to the York force with keen ambition, but her relationship with Dave had undoubtedly taken the edge off that. They were thinking of a lifelong commitment.

Bob told them what he could of their new boss, drawing on his memories of Hallam at the final assessment all those months before. He filled in some more time by telling them about the people who had gathered to welcome Hallam, and what the canteen staff had put out for them to eat. Before long, as he could think of nothing else to say and the excitement had died down a little, he reminded them that Hallam would probably be visiting soon to take possession of his office and meet them in person, and that ordinary work ought to start again.

'We had better tidy up a bit,' said

Jenny Wren. 'We want to make a good impression.'

'You will do that by being up to date with your work,' said Bob tartly as he saw Jenny pull out a duster from one of her desk drawers. 'Get your in-trays emptied.'

Everyone began to sort out their desks and Bob retired to his office. Once he had gone, several of the female staff surreptitiously borrowed dusters from the cupboard used by the cleaners.

It was now a relief to be on his own. He remembered he also had work to do.

As the hot afternoon wore on and Hallam did not put in an appearance, Bob was several times interrupted by people asking for guidance properly to be given by the new superintendent, people coming in from other departments not his own and expecting to find Hallam already at work. Bob could only assume they had been saving these problems up, so that they would have something to take to the new man. It was rubbing salt into the wound. Prickly and vaguely antagonistic, unlike himself, Bob said again and again, 'You need to see Detective Superintendent Hallam about that.'

'It will take him a few days to settle in,' one officer protested.

'True. Well, I'll do what I can for you. But as soon as he's available, you'll have to check with him.'

Still the atmosphere wasn't normal. Everyone jumped when they heard a footstep in the corridor or a door opening, or when the phone rang. It might be Hallam! Heads turned, only to turn back to their work in disappointment.

The superintendent had two offices: a small, workmanlike box at Fulford, and the larger, more luxurious one in the old building on Clifford Street. Bob had spent ninety per cent of his time there. As time went by that afternoon and Hallam had still not arrived, Bob began to realise it was on the cards that the new man might prefer to spend most of his time at the Fulford HQ.

Bob had brought down his map of York from the upper office and now he fastened it to the cork panel on the wall. It showed a scatter of coloured pins, each where in recent weeks an attack on a woman had taken place. He'd pushed them home before rolling it but some had come adrift and he repositioned them carefully.

'I expect I'll be taken off this job,' he remarked to Dave Smart.

'I expect so, boss,' said Dave.

'You are so bloody comforting.'

'That's the way it goes.'

'We need some offender-profiling on this one. Look at this pattern. All the early incidents were in the Acomb area and now they've started in Huntington.'

'Moved house,' said Dave.

'Yeah. Looks like.'

'You'll have to ask if you can get someone in, do some research. Could save us a lot of time.'

'I'll do that.'

Bob had always been conscious, in his months as acting detective superintendent, that he *was* only 'acting' the grade. He had never felt the full authority vested in the appointed officer to the post. It was galling to realise that Hallam would almost certainly be able to do much more than he had been able to do, himself. He'll throw his weight about, thought Bob. Then reminded himself that it wouldn't matter what Hallam did, if the result was catching the pervert who was carrying out these crimes.

'We had a month in between,' he remarked to his staff, meaning a month without attacks. A month during which the attacker had moved house, time in which he had orientated himself to his new area, found out the secret places where he could hide, where he could keep watch and spy out the land. A month to reconnoitre.

2

DCI Southwell's life alternated between the rhythms of work and home. Work was the weft of his fabric, a busy shuttle weaving his days across the long, strong, underlying warp threads of his private life.

The Southwell home was in Clifton, a suburb to the north of the city. Based on an old village, it still had a village green where horses often grazed. The green was ornamented by an elaborate Victorian-style horse-trough, also a small brick building which was once a 'booster-station' for an early tramway, but was now a public toilet. There were trees on the green and it was surrounded by low white railings. The inhabitants of Clifton were proud of their area and its historical associations. Their only big problem was the heavy traffic which pounded northwards through their little shopping centre up to the traffic lights at the corner of the green, then either left over the River Ouse via Clifton Bridge or onward, north still, towards Herriot country and all that lay beyond.

The Southwells lived in a four-bed-roomed semi-detached house, built in 1960, on Ouse Avenue between the green and the river, and it was always a relief to Bob to reach home.

His wife Linda was a pretty woman now in her thirties. She wore her dark soft hair very short and her clothes were usually jeans and trainers, with casual tops varying according to the weather. Sometimes she took over Bob's old shirts. Bob liked it when she put on an attractive dress with a floaty skirt, stockings and high heels, but he saw her point that her normal wear was more practical. All the same, he enjoyed the revelation when she did dress up, the reminder of their younger days before children and gardens.

On this particular day, Linda knew what he must be feeling. She had thought of little else. All the time she was getting their children, Paul and Susan, off to school, doing the shopping, giving the children their midday meal, seeing them off to school again, going into the garden and mowing the lawn, making preparations for the evening meal—all the time, she had been thinking about Bob and what sort of day he must be having.

By two o'clock she was worn out by her thoughts and when a knock came on the door she welcomed the diversion. Through the front window she saw a battered old Morris car parked in the drive. As she went to answer the knock she could see an outline through the glass panel, the outline of a middle-aged woman, figure thickened by the years, topped by a thatch of wiry, greying hair. Linda knew before swinging the door open that this was an acquaintance she had been hoping to see more of and know better.

'Miss Grindal, how nice!' she exclaimed. 'Do come in. Can I give you a cup of tea? What are you doing in Clifton, pushing leaflets through letter-boxes?'

Lucy Grindal, whose father was one of the Canons of York Minster, smiled and came in as requested.

'Funnily enough I do do other things sometimes,' she said, 'apart from leaflet delivery, which is more interesting than you might think, and don't you call me Lucy, nowadays?'

Lucy was what is known as a character. She had never worked at a paid job, but worked as hard, if not harder, without one. Apart from looking after her father, who was involved in all sorts of committees as well as his practical work for destitute and desperate young men, she raised money for the church and for various charities. She did this by the usual labour-intensive methods of jumble sales, displays of crafts, concerts of early music, Victorian music hall evenings, and anything else she could think of. Quite often this involved pushing leaflets through letter-boxes, as Linda had suggested. For Lucy's recreation and pleasure she bred dachshunds and one could be seen now, poking his head as far as he could out of the small space Lucy had left open at the top of the car window.

'Is that Prince Rupert? Do bring him in,' said Linda.

A second head appeared beside Prince Rupert's.

'Clementina Crosspatch there too?' added Linda. 'Well, why not. Bring them both in, Lucy. I can't bear to see them cooped up in a car on a hot day like this.'

'If you are sure ...'

'Yes, I am.'

'Well, thank you very much, my dear. It is good of you.'

The two dogs accepted Linda's offer of a bowl of water and then flopped down on the coolness of the kitchen floor.

'You will take a cup of tea, Lucy?' asked Linda.

'With pleasure.'

Lucy hovered in the kitchen doorway as Linda, casual in her jeans, stripy top and sandals of fine leather strips, walked round the dogs, put on the kettle and set a tray.

'It is nice to catch you on your own,' said the older woman. 'Easier to talk, although your children are darlings.'

Linda laughed. 'That's true. It is lovely to be able to socialise a bit without them.'

'What did you do before, Linda?' asked Lucy.

'Before having children? I worked in an office. From leaving tech college until I was twenty-seven. Bob and I had been married three years then, got on our feet a bit, and decided the time had come to have our family. We were lucky, I got pregnant almost straight away.'

'And you haven't the urge to go out to work?'

'No fear!' Linda laughed. 'There's a girl next door—not joined on to us, that's Tom Churchyard—'

'I know Tom,' said Lucy.

'The other side, our front doors are opposite. There's a young couple with a baby, she put him in the nursery at about two months, he's nearly one now. She is always so harrassed, dashing to drop him off before work, dashing to shop and pick him up after work, dashing to cook the evening meal—her life must be a misery.

Anyway, I couldn't stand it, Lucy.'

'I don't blame you.'

'Surely—' Linda was on her hobby horse, there was no stopping her—'surely the most important task the world has to offer is bringing up your children?'

'There can't be any other situation of such absolute dependence and trust. It is awe-inspiring. I don't know how I would have dared tackle motherhood, if the opportunity had arisen in my life, Linda.'

The younger woman gave her an affectionate glance and reached out a hand to pat her arm. 'You'd have been a super mum, Lucy.'

Lucy smiled and changed the subject. 'Your house is very pretty. Fresh and light. And you are always so busy. Homemade scones, aren't they?'

The women moved into the through room, where Linda put the tray on her coffee table. The patio window was open on to the green fragrance of the garden.

'What are those enormous plants?' asked Lucy. 'Surely not nicotiana?'

'Yes, *Nicotiana sylvestris*. It is actually flowering. I've been longing for this large variety but although the seed comes up like mustard and cress, the plants are usually just ready to flower when the first frosts come. This year I sowed them extra early.'

'I'm very impressed,' said Lucy. 'Have you always gardened?'

'No. The gardening just grew, if you'll forgive the expression.'

'I like the colour scheme. All green and white here, and pale pinks, creams and mauves in your front garden.'

'I will design your summer bedding for your garden next year, if you like, Lucy,' said Linda, starting all unknowingly her new career.

'You have an artistic eye,' said Lucy. 'So lovely to come here and see your garden. I'm afraid mine is all roses and grass, and big old trees. The idea of you designing my summer bedding—in all fairness I had better tell you I've never bothered with it in the past—almost makes me forget why I came.'

'You don't need a reason, it is always nice to see you,' said Linda, putting cups and saucers out on the coffee table. She liked the older woman. Mind, in the mood she'd been in, she would have welcomed almost anyone.

'On such an idyllic occasion why does horror have to intrude?' said Lucy.

'Horror?'

'What are we to do about this man who is attacking women?' Lucy's words were a discord in the lazy heat of the late summery afternoon.

'Do you think there is anything we can do?'

'In any situation there is usually something one can do, and feel better for doing it, even if it turns out to be futile. As your husband is in the police force I thought you might have some thoughts about it, some advice to give.'

'He doesn't discuss his job with me, I'm afraid. He is more likely to talk to you, if you approached him officially and asked for advice.'

'My ideas haven't crystallised to that

extent. You too must have been thinking about it, Linda. I did have a vague idea about self-defence classes for women.'

Linda looked at her. 'I'll tell you what, Lucy. My friend Julie would like to be in on this discussion. That is the very thing she mentioned to me the other day. Julia Brandsby, I think you know her. Let me give her a ring. If she's free I'll ask her to pop round and join us. She only lives a few minutes' way away, in a flat at the Dutch House on the bridge.'

As Lucy sipped her tea she could hear Linda's voice on the phone, and guessed from her responses that Julia was agreeing to come. Lucy tried to remember what she knew about Julia Brandsby. An embroidery specialist, that was it. A voluntary guide in York Minster when she could fit it in, she had also written articles about the Minster embroideries. It was some time since they had met, and Lucy guessed that Julia was too busy at the moment to carry out voluntary guiding at the Minster. There had been that dreadful murder, too, at the Dutch House complex.

'She'll be here in two minutes,' said Linda, coming back and sitting down. 'She will ride round on that moped of hers.'

'She's very brave to ride it in today's traffic,' said Lucy. 'It is quite bad enough in a car.'

Linda had seen Lucy driving the ancient Morris. It was a sight to fill anyone with dread and apprehension. Usually the view through the car's back window was obstructed by bouncing dachshunds. The car itself was surely achieving antique status. It was amazing Lucy was allowed on the road. Linda felt less worried about Julia on her moped.

The moped transported Julia Brandsby round in two minutes flat, and she entered the long cool room still removing her helmet, which she put on the floor. Like Linda, Julia had short dark hair, but whereas Linda's was soft and feathery, Julia's was stronger and crisper, cut to fall in two curves on to her cheeks at the front and almost shingled at the back. In age she was between the other two; her only child, Adam, was now at university.

'Lovely to see you, Lucy,' she said, coming over to shake Lucy Grindal's hand. Lucy has smartened herself up lately, she thought. Aloud she said, 'May I tell you how much I like your dress?'

It was dusty pink linen with a little drawn-thread work on the bodice, and Lucy wore a charming pink and white shell cameo with it.

'Why, thank you, Julia. You go for the embroidery, of course.'

'Yes, it's perfect—just enough and not too much.'

'Do you know why I'm here today?'

'Yes. Linda told me on the phone about your idea of self-defence classes. What can we do to get them doing?'

'I'm so glad you think we should.'

'Definitely.'

'Find a teacher, I suppose,' said Linda.

'And premises. It would be easiest if either the local authority or the WEA organised a class.'

'What does WEA stand for? Forgive my ignorance,' said Linda.

'Do I rate a cuppa, Linda?' asked Julia.

Linda went for another cup. 'Scone?' she asked.

'WEA? Workers' Educational Association,' said Lucy, answering Linda's previous question and taking a scone as well. 'It was started in the days when working people left school at thirteen or fourteen. There was a great longing for education. The organisation still offers people what they want, but the subjects tend to be more unusual.'

'I know,' said Julia 'I'm often asked to do lectures for them. An ordinary creative embroidery class would be organised by the local authority, but a class called "Embroidery in the Medieval Period" would be WEA.'

'So what's "Self-defence for Women"?' asked Linda.

'Local authority, definitely,' said Julia.

'Yes, but the threat is now, and both those bodies fix their classes ages in advance. How can we get something going now—straight away?' said Lucy Grindal.

'Do it privately,' said Julia thoughtfully. 'Advertise in the local papers.'

'Once we've found a teacher and a hall suitable for the purpose,' added Linda. 'I'm not sure what form it would take, this self-defence. Would it be like karate?'

They were all silent for a minute, none of them sure what one could do when attacked from behind by blows on the head. Then Julia raised another issue.

'Would we be allowed to advertise anything as only for women? Wouldn't that be sex discrimination?'

'Probably. But the so-called Ripper only attacks women.'

'I don't think we should use that term, Lucy,' said Linda, being the policeman's wife. 'It is emotive. This man hasn't done any ripping. It is a much milder case, though frightening, I agree.'

'You are right, Linda,' said Lucy. 'It only provokes fear. I won't use it in future. I wouldn't have thought of it if it was not already in the air. But about a venue—there is a place on Moss Street, or just off Moss Street. I know about it because dog training sessions are held there. The floor is marked out for various

42

sports. I have made tentative enquiries.'

'That sounds ideal,' said Linda. 'Could we hire it, that's the thing. And we would have to find a teacher.'

'Could be a man,' said Julia. 'The sex of the teacher wouldn't matter.'

The three women were very different but they found they made a good team.

'Why can't the United Nations get on as well as we've done?' speculated Lucy later.

The little impromptu meeting that afternoon in Linda Southwell's through room finished with Lucy Grindal agreeing to be chief organiser, as the one with most experience of such organisation, most contacts and most time—besides, she had taken the initiative in the first place. (Julia had also thought of it but, apart from mentioning the idea to Linda, had taken no positive action.) Julia and Linda promised their help and support. Lucy was privately sure the project would involve her in shoving more leaflets through letter-boxes.

Together they felt they had created an

Action Group, and this cheered them considerably. They felt more in control of their lives, and as though the ordinary woman-in-the-suburb, as Linda put it, could really do something to change matters.

'I'd better go,' Lucy said, after three o'clock. 'Leaflet through letter-box time. Well, not really. I'm teasing you, Linda. Preparing meal time. Come on, dogs. In the car. Don't bother to come out, either of you.'

But they did, of course.

'Nice, isn't she?' said Linda as they watched the car lurch out of the driveway.

'Pretty shrewd cookie,' said Julia. 'Self-help. We need more of that in today's world.'

Linda felt different after the afternoon's discussion. She felt more self-possessed, more an individual. Being a wife and mother gave her little time for herself. Now she had grown, for a while, into a mature self-contained member of society. She had not thought of either husband or children for an hour.

Julia Brandsby, who stayed a little longer gossiping with Linda, had also gone when the Southwell children arrived home from school. Paul and Susan asked if they could eat their meal in the tent in the back garden.

'Only if you help,' Linda bargained as usual. They were learning about fending for themselves, even if at first they had lived on burnt sausages and nearly-cold baked beans. This afternoon Linda helped by cutting bread, which Susan buttered thickly, while Paul cut slices from a cold chicken, with his tongue between his front teeth. Then the children disappeared into the garden, to sit and eat in the green cool of the tent, leaving Linda to prepare her own meal and Bob's.

She had bought his favourite meat, steak, and with it they were having chips, and mixed salad. Somehow she guessed he would be home promptly, but was waiting until he arrived before cooking the main course. She whipped some cream for the summer pudding which was in the fridge. Linda believed in the therapeutic power over the human male of an interesting pudding served with cream. As she worked she became anxious again, wondering how the day had gone for him.

She was right in her guess. Bob arrived at five thirty. She looked at his face. Strained. His greeting was quiet.

'He's arrived, then?' she asked.

'Kept us waiting,' he replied, 'and didn't show up at Clifford Street all afternoon.'

Somehow Linda did not ask anything else. She did not mention her own activities during the day, because at the moment he would obviously not be interested, although normally he liked to hear her chatter.

By the end of the next day she was feeling even more worried. Surely by now Bruno Hallam must have taken over at Clifford Street? That was why she spent half the morning messing about making sherry trifle. Not quite half the morning. Three-quarters of an hour, anyway—but it seemed like ages.

Bob arrived home on time again, and kissed her fondly. As always her senses were on the alert, judging how he was

46

by touch, taste and smell as well as sight and hearing. Tense, she concluded, but not too unhappy. She detected a little relief. She put on her cooking apron and moved back into the kitchen as Bob greeted his children. They had eaten in the tent again, and were now sitting on the floor of the through room watching television. Linda hoped it would keep them quiet while the grown-ups had their meal. She was anxious for her talk with Bob, but waited until they had eaten their first course and his eyes lit up at the sight of the trifle.

'How was it then?' she asked.

He didn't pretend not to know what she was talking about.

3

Nearly all day he had been on edge waiting for Bruno Hallam to arrive at Clifford Street. When he did come, Bob had plenty of warning of his approach. It seemed to his listening ear that Hallam stopped beside every single member of staff and held a long conversation. By the time he arrived at Bob's office, the new detective superintendent was beaming with bonhomie and Bob was shaking with nerves. Why did this man have such an effect on him?

'Good to see you, Bob,' said Hallam, holding out his hand for the second time in two days, and firmly clasping Bob's. 'Sorry to have been so long getting round. But I know you are doing a good job here and there's been a lot to grasp.'

'Yes,' said Bob. 'Can I show you your office in this building? It's just upstairs.'

'Thanks.'

The two men went and inspected the office.

'I expect to be spending most of my time at Fulford,' said Hallam, 'but it's good to have this to come to when necessary. Now put me in the picture with the enquiry you're on, Bob. These attacks on women. We'll go down again to the nerve centre. Floor below, next to your office, eh? With all those maps and charts?'

For a second Bob felt that loss of self-confidence again, but he pulled himself up sharply. He knew his job backwards, there was no need to feel like that.

'It began,' he explained, 'with two attacks on women in the Acomb area, one of those York suburbs which began as separate villages.'

'Most cities have done this, haven't they?' remarked Hallam. 'Flowed out and round isolated settlements.'

'Yes. Acomb has the remnant of a village green and its parish church has a very large graveyard. There is still the old centre and the feeling of natural growth over time, in spite of the modern estates. The women of Acomb were worried by those first attacks, but they weren't generally known in the city. Separately, a week apart, two women walking down a quiet lane had been knocked unconscious. The first woman had suffered nothing more, but the second had her clothing disarranged. It was not until the third attack that we realised it was becoming a series.'

'That is the usual pattern of these things,' said Hallam.

'I became involved at that point.'

Bob visualised clearly the moment: the weather, the room, his acting DCI Dave Smart standing before him, the way he himself had said, 'Three attacks?'

'We realised it was possible that there had been more than three; the culprit might have attacked others who didn't contact the police.'

'True,' said Hallam, looking at the map where the sites of attacks were marked by pins.

'We had the three women in at the station and took careful statements and as much detail as we could get, particularly descriptions of the man. Dates, times, places. David Smart was in charge. His report was on its way to me when we had news of the fourth attack. By now of course the Acomb police had been thoroughly briefed about procedure and the local newspaper had unfortunately got hold of it. Our publicity officer put out a short statement, and the women of the area were warned to be careful. One result was two more women coming forward to state that they, too, had been attacked, but hadn't said anything to anybody about it. One must have been the first he tried, his blows were inept and she had a good look at him, but she wasn't very hot on description. The other was later, occurring between the original third and fourth. He knocked her out all right, but that was all. Then everything went quiet.'

'For how long?'

'A month. Of course we all hoped that we had heard the last of it. Then the first episode at Huntington made us escalate our enquiries. I became actively involved and we put up these maps and calendar. We sent out a public appeal asking the community to report anything suspicious that could have a bearing. For the second time there was the feature which has become characteristic, the disarrangement of the clothing.'

'The whole town seems to be in the grip of panic.'

'People can't help remembering another series of attacks, only twenty-five miles away. Attacks which also started with disarrangement of clothing only, but which led to murders. People living in York were terrified, although in fact there were no cases in the city. A pall of fear seemed to hang over everything, I was told. In fact I was still in Harrogate at the time, it was the same there. As soon as the Sutcliffe case came back into people's memories, there was no holding the irrational emotion. It could have turned into mass panic. We have been directing our efforts ever since towards avoiding that, asking the media to co-operate. The number of reported cases went up.

Girls and women of all ages remembered things that had happened to themselves or their friends, incidents which had not been reported. When the reports came to a round dozen I was agitating for a photofit, but the details were vague, and at that time we couldn't produce anything usable. The artist came up with an "impression" which we did use. The sex side of the attacks was becoming clearer. We issued advice to women, "Don't walk in unlit areas, report anything suspicious, walk with someone else if possible."'

'You are right about the memory of the Sutcliffe case. Still very clear in people's minds. I have seen references to the Ripper in the local newspapers. Very unfortunate. The word is so emotive.'

'It goes without saying that we didn't start the use of that word.'

'No one would ever think we had. At least I hope they wouldn't think us quite that stupid. Any other police areas involved?'

'We published an intelligence bulletin

outlining the attacks, with the usual info, descriptions, the artist's impression, times, dates. It went to all the regional forces, and to all prisons.'

'Any results from that?'

'No. Not yet. Could still happen. Our own intelligence office is doing its best.'

'I saw them earlier as I was coming through to you. One policeman and one civilian full time on that.'

'That is the usual number, but other staff are available if they want extra help. They have been calling on help.'

'Where are the attacks centred now?'

'Huntington until a week ago, then it suddenly fell quiet there. Random attacks are taking place, in the city centre where there haven't been any before, and in the inner suburbs.'

'Any copy-cats?'

'I'm sure of it. There are several which don't quite fit the pattern.'

'Any clothing missing from the victims?'

'Not so far.'

'How serious is the physical damage?'

'He's become good at rendering them

unconscious. We thought at first he was using a bit of loaded hosepipe, but we now feel it's more likely to be the good old idea of a weighted sock.'

'A cosh of some sort, in other words.'

'Yes.'

'Have you taken any outer clothing and sent it for forensic examination?'

'Many of the cases have been classed as minor, and you know how tight budgeting is at present, sir.'

'The series seems to be pretty well established. What you are saying is, it needs a policy decision. Well, I'll give you authority for the expenditure here and now, Bob. The next case, we take outer clothing for examination at the Wetherby lab.'

Hallam spent some time reading intently through the notes on the case.

'You didn't mention you had mounted plain-clothes observation,' he remarked to Bob.

'It was of very limited use.'

'At present the attacks are random?'

'Yes, sir.'

'As soon as we get two consecutive in a place, I suggest plain-clothes observation again.'

'I did have that in mind.'

'Don't delay on account of the overtime. I will back you up.'

Bob had tried not to sound possessive. He had had no doubt Hallam would be taking over. After all, there was nothing more important on, at that time. But Hallam's most recent remarks gave him the impression it might not be like that.

'I'm proud to have you on my team, Bob,' said Hallam, and Bob thought, Here comes the *but* ...

'In fact ...' Hallam paused. 'I'm going to ask you to continue in command of this enquiry. I'll keep a watching brief, but there's no reason for me to take over. Quite a lot of issues at Fulford I'd like to deal with straight away. Is that okay with you?'

'Perfectly, sir,' said Bob.

'Bruno's the name, Bob, when we are on our own.'

He left and Bob wondered what urgent

issues at Fulford took precedence over actual bodily harm to the women of York, but he was too happy at retaining control to worry about it.

The effect of Bruno Hallam on the Clifford Street staff was electric. In one short visit he seemed to have won them over. When they heard that he intended to fight the planned closure of the staff social club, they were more supportive of him than ever.

Bob did not share in the warm enthusiasm, but he felt that his instinctive antagonism had decreased. When Linda put her question on that night he even went so far as to say, 'It doesn't look as though Hallam will be too unbearable. I expect I have to make the best of a bad job. He's left me in control of the attacker enquiry. He spoke to everyone individually, went round the building, made a good impression. He didn't throw his weight about too much.'

'Oh, Bob, that is good!'

'You know, Lindy-Lou, I've been thinking. I've got to try to overcome my feelings about Hallam. He's here and I'll have to make the best of it or my life will be a misery.'

'Yes. I'm sure that's right.'

In his euphoria about staying in charge, Bob was overlooking all the irritation Bruno Hallam had in fact caused him. The aura of ... well, wealth almost. Hallam had as usual been wearing a suit of deep grey, and Bob had noticed the hand-finished lapels, the white good-quality shirt, the plain cuff links which still shouted 'high carat gold', and, last but not least, the faint aroma of expensive aftershave and—yes, he was certain—very good cigars. Bob had also noticed the effect Hallam had on the female staff.

It was not going to be easy, but Bob began to fight his antipathy. He realised that Hallam was a type he had not come into contact with before, and so was difficult to sum up. That was the source of the problem. He determined, as he tackled the sherry trifle, to find good things to say about Hallam every night, to Linda. As long as he and his new boss kept out of each other's way it was not going to be too difficult.

The attacker had by now acquired the sinister nickname of the 'Ripper' not because he ripped bodies, but because he ripped clothes from his victims. They often suffered small cuts in the process. Whoever started to use the name for this new attacker did a disservice to York. There were so many fears, so much freight on this of all names, that the air had become thick with terror.

Elderly ladies in back streets were afraid to put out milk bottles on their front doorsteps in case they were hit from behind as they bent over to lower the bottle to the ground. Young women taking their children to the park were careful to go in twos. Middle-aged women alone in their houses locked the doors at front and back before settling to watch their television in the evening.

And all this in spite of the attacker's known methods and chosen *modus operandi*, of which most of the details were published in the local papers. He had no record of the kind of attacks they feared. He only attacked women in the open air, away from houses. They had to be alone and on foot in quiet streets or open spaces, but not *too* quiet.

On one typical evening a woman was being driven home by a friend from a girls' night out.

'Do you dare to go down there on your own?' asked the friend, peering into the darkness of an isolated track.

'Yes,' came the common-sense reply. 'If he was waiting for someone to rape or bonk on the head down my lane, he'd have had a helluva long wait. He'll have given up and gone home.'

In spite of this the driver shuddered and insisted on driving down the unmade-up lane, all pot-holes and puddles, and waiting until her friend had unlocked the door and given a wave.

The fear was not rational. It did not depend on the number of related attacks, bearing the same hallmark. It was a miasma over the city. Bob was puzzled that Hallam did not wish instantly to take over the enquiry and, by some dazzling performance, solve it.

4

There was reason in the resurrected 'Ripper' fears, for there were similarities. So far the worst that had happened was that women had been left stretched unconscious on the ground, their clothing pulled down and up, ripped or torn, showing the world their breasts, hips and private parts in a strange and humiliating fashion. But beyond the knockout blows there had been no further violence, and beyond the hurts incurred during the rough disarrangement of clothing no sexual damage. It was assumed by the public that the man—for surely it must be a man, no question—had not yet carried out his full purpose: rape ... torture ... disfigurement ... wounding ... murder ...

Many of the attacks had not gone as far as unconsciousness. When the attacker had mistimed or misjudged distance so that the victim caught only a glancing blow and reacted to protect herself, a running figure was all they could describe. Some had realised they were being followed, and turned round. From such sightings a picture was building up of a man both tall and short, fat and thin, young and old, bald and hairy.

One morning at the beginning of October Bob Southwell called Dave Smart into his office and said, 'I think we had better contact the colleges and the university, Dave, and discuss security with them. Some of their students will know about what has been happening, but they will have young people coming from all over the country and overseas as well.'

'Do you want me to organise it, boss?'

'Yes. Get someone to draft out some ideas for them—prepare a handout of some kind. Also contact the top brass and arrange a visit. Low key, no publicity, but if for instance an overseas student should be assaulted, I don't want anyone to be able to say that we hadn't warned them.'

It was a week before the draft handout was ready for Bob's approval.

'It's good,' he congratulated the staff. Then to Dave, 'I think I will visit the university myself, Mr Smart. It would be a courtesy and they will appreciate it.'

Bob wanted an excuse to get out of the office for a bit.

The original ancient city of York is, on the whole, a flat place, not much above sea level, apart from the slightly higher area crowned by the Minster. This height is partly due to the steadily rising debris of human life and activity, added to the small rise in the land from the river level.

There is, though, a glacial moraine at a little distance from the core of the city. It is broken and rudimentary after so many centuries, but a long fragment lying from west to east shelters the university from the weather and provides a sunny south-facing slope for the elegance and airiness of a brilliantly conceived and dramatic campus.

The hot weather went on very late, that

year. At the campus at Heslington, the new students were arriving for Fresher Week. They had come from all over the world to live among buildings still as surprising and varied as when they were built in the sixties. The landscaping, with the lake, the fountain, the loving details of the hard surfaces, the sculptures and bas reliefs, the living trees and shrubs, the squirrels and waterfowl, was as delightful to the eye. There was still about the place a free, uplifting openness, an airy, breezy quality, in the campus designed next to the old red brick of the Tudor Heslington Hall.

Bob Southwell knew the campus well, and liked it. After parking his car he strode energetically towards his conference with the security team. Also invited to be present were those provosts of colleges who wished to be involved.

It was a warm afternoon with a blue sky tender over the rooftops. Everywhere along the covered walkways which joined one building to another, people were strolling with obvious pleasure and a sense of holiday. Mostly they were small family

65

groups, student and parents.

Bob did notice one person on her own, a tall girl with long blonde hair blowing in the breeze. It was difficult not to notice Angela Morton. She looked striking and her face was thoughtful. Bob felt sorry to be leaving the open air and going inside to the conference. It was pleasant to watch these youngsters, he decided.

Angela had not noticed him. She was glad that she was alone to discover the place. The taxi had dropped her near her hall of residence and she had found her room and left her luggage in it, then come out to explore.

As Angela walked along one of the covered walkways she was taking in all the details of her surroundings, the bicycles leaning against the uprights and the chalked notices above her head on the crossbeams of the canopy: *BLOOD WEDDING Thurs, Fri, Sat, Sun, Week 2, 7.30 Drama Barn.* There were paper stickers, *CHRISTIS York University's Christian magazine. Join us at the Freshers Fair Saturday Week 0,* and on a support post of the canopy, *York University*

Our bodies Our lives Our choice Pro Choice Society. Each O of this last notice had a tiny cross beneath it, making the letter into the symbol of femininity. It was this that stuck in Angela's mind, Our *choice*. Choice. She wondered whether one really had any. She felt her life had been decided for her.

After a last admiring glance in her direction, the tall detective forgot Angela and turned right into a doorway in the cliff-like side of a block of building.

At the same moment, Angela veered from the paved way on to the grass. She walked crunchily over the shells of horse chestnut seeds lying in small drifts at every ridge of ground. An old man walked slowly nearby and bent now and then, his eye quick as a boy's to spot the whole seed, his fingers swift to pick it up. As Angela watched, he split one open and revealed a perfect conker and on his face was a look of delight as he put it in his pocket. Angela looked down and searched too, and found a seed half open, the prickly shell brown, spiked as if it was a tiny mine, packed not with destructive explosive but with the explosion of life which might become a towering chestnut tree. The conker was silky in her hand, gleaming brown mahogany, magical and perfect. She, too, put it in her pocket.

The busy road was crossed by foot-bridges and she found the stair that led up to one of them, a double stair like the entrance to a stately home. It was planted on either side with small trees whose branches formed a roof, from which the large pointed leaves hung vertically. As she climbed one side of the stair to the bridge, stood for a moment without crossing the road, then went down the other side of the stair, Angela thought it was like walking through the Chinese design on a willow pattern plate. With its shallow steps the stair was a three-dimensional treasure and she wondered if she would walk over it with a lover, a friend, a group of friends, when the canopy was bare of leaves, when they budded, when they were a thick green glory, when they turned as now into pure gold, when they fell.

She walked by the lake and could hear

the water lapping, the children on roller blades, the male students on skateboards and the low murmurs of conversation. Reaching the back of the old mellow red manor house where three young men were playing with a floating, spinning frisbee, she found herself humming.

It was only when she left the family groups and was walking back up the stairs to her room that the solitary Angela was suddenly engulfed by a small black cloud of loss and longing and she felt herself call out, 'Daddy!' as tears rushed into her eyes. The cry was silent. For a moment she stood with her eyes closed enduring the pain. When she opened them again the tears were not visible. A glance upwards and downwards told her that no one had noticed, there was no one in view on the staircase, although there were people higher and lower in the building—she could hear their voices and footsteps. It was strange, she thought, that the pain was as sharp as ever after so many years. A few moments passed. She walked upwards. Angela had not seen her real father for ten years. The divorce between her parents had torn her apart. Her mother had taken to saying unpleasant things to her about her father, trying to turn the child against him. How was she to know what was the truth? Yes, on the last of his access visits (which had been growing rarer and rarer) she had looked at him through her mother's eyes and seen him with hatred. Then the long separation had begun. Now, so many years after the event, she wondered if she would even recognise him again. Only now and then, like today, she was suddenly overcome with a longing for him so intense, so physical, that it hurt. Almost more than she could bear. 'Daddy!' she whispered again as she climbed upwards. You are my father, I am your child, why are we apart?

When Bob Southwell came out of that door again, an hour and a quarter later, he looked round for the long-haired blonde girl. He thought that when his own little daughter was nineteen or so she might look very like that girl, and he wondered whether he would be bringing Susan to start her first year at university. Well, he could dream, couldn't he? On that day he would be a proud man.

'How did it go, boss?' asked Dave Smart when the two of them were relaxing over a pint in one of the town centre pubs. Bob preferred a standard bitter and Dave had begun to favour stout. Bob waited for a second as he drank his first long swallow before he replied.

'Lovely place,' he said. 'The security staff were fine. The provosts were a bit quirky. Academics tend to be quirky. Use words only another academic can understand.'

'Don't live in the real world,' said Dave.

'Charming, though. Really civilised company, not like most of the men we meet. One of them, Dr Keith Blow, would charm the birds off the trees. He was doing all right with the only female provost and the waitress who brought the coffee as well. Courtesy, Dave. Oodles of it.'

'Women's libbers object to courtesy,' was Dave's opinion. 'Don't like the door held open or you to offer them a seat on the bus.'

'If you offered me a seat on the bus I'd take it, Dave.'

'There's special seats for old age pensioners, boss.'

By the time the university term really started, a process of appraisal was going on among the new undergraduates. Not so much between staff and students, although there was that, or would be that, once lectures and seminars really got into their stride, but between the students themselves. They discovered those in adjoining rooms in the dormitory blocks, or spoke to someone in the canteen—perhaps sharing a table—and felt an affinity which might turn into friendship, or an antipathy which might turn into enmity.

A few of the older male students lounged about in the Students' Union and other informal meeting places, eyeing up the new girls. There was one who stood out, even in that display of radiant skins and firm young bodies. One girl who —slightly taller than average, athletic, walking with an unusual free grace—drew their attention.

The men couldn't help noticing Angela. The girls noticed her too, and reserved their opinions. Her hair was naturally flaxen. It shone. It flowed smooth and straight on to her shoulders. When fascinated eyes moved downwards they saw a slender athletic body and fabulous legs. Even before seeing her face the men gave her nine out of ten. She wore shorts, trainers, T-shirt, and a sports top tied round her shoulders. There was something too in the personality of this quiet, reflective girl which immediately made her distinctive.

A day or two after the start of term proper, Angela was in the restaurant at Langwith College and had collected a meal on a tray.

'I'm Jessica,' said a short dark girl, coming to the same table with a loaded tray. 'Can I join you?'

Angela smiled, moved her papers to a chair, and closed her book. She could go on with that any time.

'Aren't you reading English?' Jessica went on eagerly. 'Are you going to the lecture at two? Are you joining the

Women's Group?'

'I'm doing English and expect I'm going to the lecture.'

There had been a choice: 'Seventeenth-Century Literature', 'American Literature 1890-1945', or 'Victorians'.

Angela and Jessica found they had both chosen 'Victorians'. The first of a series to be given by Jane Barlow was 'The Victorian Period'. The same tutor was to give five lectures altogether. It was unusual for them to take place in the afternoon, but today's 2 p.m. was an exception to the usual 10.15 a.m.

'There are two lecturers this afternoon,' said Jessica, checking with her diary. 'I expect we have a tea break between them. No, we don't. The second is Karl Hanson, talking about "Victorian Hero Cults—Arthur and Camelot". It starts the same time the first one finishes.'

Jessica stuffed some salad into her mouth and then said in parenthesis, 'I always choose vegetarian here.' She picked up a leaflet from the table and passed it to Angela.

'ARE YOU A FEMINIST?' asked the leaflet in large caps, and in smaller caps, WHAT DOES FEMINISM MEAN TO YOU? CAN MEN BE FEMINISTS?' Angela noticed that the headline lettering had an almost handwritten quality, but decided it was likely to be computer generated rather than scanned in. The text continued in lower-case letters. Angela read slowly, between bites of food and assessment of her companion.

Women's Group, she read, *is for all women, whether you love women or men or both, wear dungarees or dresses, whatever your political views, whether you feel you are 'political' or not, whether you've been to Women's Group before or not, so come along and have your say! All women are welcome so please come and let us know what you think!*

'I might come along to this sometime, Jessica,' Angela said at last, smiling. Reaching into her pocket she pulled out a little bundle of canvas and threads, unrolled it and began to put a few stitches in. She leaned back in her chair and looked utterly relaxed.

'Jess, most people call me,' said the short, dark girl. She was surprised to notice that Angela's eyes, when seen fully, were mid-brown with golden lights in them, and fringed by black lashes. Angela's eyebrows were fair but her only trace of makeup was the use of an eyebrow pencil to darken them slightly.

'Who wears dungarees, though?' went on Angela.

'They probably chose the word to alliterate with "dresses",' said Jess. 'Which block are you in? Oh! Great! So am I.'

Angela realised that here, on what she felt to be her first day of normal university life, she could already form a circle of friends. Jess was born to be a nucleus of networks. Attending the Women's Group would automatically put her, Angela, in touch with a certain set among the students. Should she drift into this or wait, consider, look around, before affiliating, or move into the first congenial thing that offered?

Jess looked at Angela, snatching short, sharp little looks between attending to her meal. She felt a desire for the friendship of this cool, self-contained girl. There would be a slight feeling of privilege, for Angela came over as withdrawn and rather special. She would not be likely to divulge what made her tick.

'What are you stitching?' she asked.

'Oh!' Angela gave a self-deprecating laugh. 'I find it very relaxing for odd moments, and we can talk at the same time. Little bits of stitching.' She held out the piece for Jessica to see. It measured about six inches by four and showed a tiny picture of a Canada goose.

'I sketched him on the campus, near the lake,' she added, 'and drew him on to canvas.'

'What will you do with it when it's finished?'

'Nothing, probably. I've a drawer full of them.'

'Why do them and put them in a drawer?' said Jess.

'I will do something with them one day,' Angela answered. 'Perhaps frame them into little pictures for presents.'

Laying the bit of needlework down on

the table, Angela picked up another leaflet and began to read it. It was the 'Daily Info' from the York University Students' Union.

'It does occur to me,' she said with a twinkle of humour, 'that if one took part fully in the life of the university, there would be little time for studying.'

'True,' said Jessica with her mouth full. 'But in our first year do we have to work hard? Are your people slave-drivers?'

Angela hesitated before replying. 'There's no pressure,' she said at last, unable to say 'my people'. He was only her stepfather, although She was her mother. No. Angela refused to call them her people. She went on, 'But I need to answer to myself—does that sound priggish?'

Jess thought it ridiculous for anyone who looked as Angela did. She shrugged. 'However it grabs you,' she said. 'I'm into *Star Wars* myself. There's a Star Wars Quiz in the Vanbrugh Bar at nine o'clock. Have some fun, why don't you? Look,' she went on more seriously, 'there's a bit of a scare on in York. Some women have been attacked lately. There's a free bus service into the city and back in the evenings. It makes sense to use it.'

'Thanks for the tip,' said Angela. 'When I'm in training I tend to go to bed early, but I'll remember.'

Leaving Jess at the outer door of the canteen, Angela walked back to her room slowly. She realised that there was far more to university life than she had anticipated. A single-sex grant-maintained school had not really prepared her for it, even though she had gone out with various young males of her own age and become used to controlling the situation. At the sixth-form college she had met much the same kind of relationships as, she envisaged, she would meet at university. During the 'year out' which she had just completed there had been a variety of situations—some happy, some confused, some difficult. She considered herself fairly experienced without having ever thought seriously about the women's movement. Hadn't equality been won?

Jess's conversation suddenly seemed to

Angela to loom, like a small cloud no bigger than a man's hand. She would spend time thinking about it. She would observe, and allow her opinion to be formed by what she saw about her. Yet Angela knew she was deceiving herself; the anger and loneliness within her, the emotional yearning which for the last years had filled her with desolation and hindered her psychic growth, would continue to cut her off from her fellow creatures as effectively as a blank wall.

At the lecture later that day Jess discovered that when Angela entered a lecture hall, almost noiseless, sat down, put her notepad on her knee and settled to listen, everyone knew she was there. A sense of occasion missing at other times became manifest.

It was the next day that Bob Southwell, returning to the office after his lunch break, strolled along King's Staith from Ouse Bridge. The original bridge had once been one of the prettiest in Europe, and many artists had painted it. The present one also had a lot of charm which most people were in too much of a hurry to notice. Bob was no expert on architecture but he liked Ouse Bridge, and the stair down to King's Staith, which was often inundated with flood water from Ouse. The pub on the Staith was used to the flooding, not that it enjoyed the experience, which usually came at least once every winter.

There were a number of cars, colourful and glittering, parked along the Staith and in the streets leading off it up towards the castle. Bob was surprised to see DI Dave Smart and DC Jenny Wren standing by one of the cars and apparently locked in each other's arms. As he strode towards them, Bob saw that the car they were standing by was Jenny's new car, and that her head was resting on Dave's chest, which she seemed to be soaking with tears.

'What's this?' asked Bob, sounding stern, as he came up to them.

Dave didn't answer. He only waved his thumb in the direction of the much-longed-for bright metallic blue new car.

'Don't usually park your car down here, do you, Jenny?' asked Bob. He had now taken in at a glance the bright red scrawl of an obscene message which obscured the windscreen. 'Let go of her, Dave,' he added.

Dave let go and Jenny, her face partly covered in her handkerchief, said with a throat full of tears, 'I'm sorry, boss.'

'Whatever happens you shouldn't make a display like that in a public place,' Bob told her, but his voice had lost its stern note.

'I don't normally park here,' she sobbed, 'but I knew there wouldn't be any magistrates around today and as I came in early it occurred to me to see if there was a space, before going as I usually do to the Lord Mayor's Walk car-park.'

'There was a space and this has happened,' said Bob.

'Yes.'

'You've been in the force long enough to be inured.'

'I thought I was tough now,' said Jenny.

'We are none of us tough when it is

personal, I suppose,' said Bob. 'This is the most crazy revolting message I've ever seen. Looks as if it's been done in paint. Do you know the bloke who did it?'

She looked surprised. 'Surely it is random—not meant for me? I thought ... just some nutter walking past ...'

'I think it is very exactly meant for you, Jen. Sorry. This is some gentleman you have upset very much indeed.'

'But how would anyone know it was my car?'

'Not difficult, if they have been watching you.'

'Stalking?'

'Not exactly. You would have been aware of that before now. Observation, not stalking. In spite of this dislike of you, and the things he intends to do to you, he thinks you will get in touch.'

'In touch?' Jenny had stopped crying and looked incredulous. 'What makes you think that?'

'He must think you will enjoy his revenge on you. Don't you see he's ended the message by putting his phone number?'

83

'There are some numbers,' said Dave. 'Oh, Lord. You're right, boss. What an idiot the man must be. Would anyone in their right mind actually leave their phone number?'

'Someone has. Don't ring it, get into contact with BT, see if you can get the address.'

'It's so—so vindictive—so foul,' said Jenny. 'How could anyone write those words on my car?'

'Get it fingerprinted, lass,' said Bob. 'And photographed. My mind is running on the attacker. This is the sort of thing, hate-filled, I can imagine him doing. We'll have this chap in for questioning. It is just possible that this might be a breakthrough.'

'You mean he could be the Ripper?'

'Jenny! You're in enough hot water as it is without using that word! We do not refer to him as that!'

'The Attacker.' Jenny found that her tears had dried. Although she was feeling just as upset, and her heart seemed to have shrivelled and become cold inside her, the tears had gone. She could now look at her car dispassionately, as an incident in the unending wave of car crime, not as her baby defaced. She had been so proud of it. Not any more. Even when the words were cleaned away she was afraid she would still see them.

'Come on,' said Bob, conscious of the time. 'You must organise fingerprinting and other scene of crime activity. Then I want you to go through your recent cases and see if there's anyone who might hold a grudge. Dave will give you the address as soon as he has it. You'll have the highest grade attention. Normally the job would only rate a detective constable.'

'You really think that I have done something—that this is personal, not random? But on what grounds?'

'My grounds? Hunch,' said Bob.

'Experience,' said Dave.

Later, Bob said quietly to Dave, 'You had better not undertake the interview. Delegate it. You are personally involved. Thinking of Jenny's reaction might make you lose your temper.'

'I do realise, boss.'

By the end of the afternoon DCI Smart had found out the name and address of the person who was renting a telephone line with the number, the number which was scrawled at the end of the obscene message written in scarlet paint on Jenny Wren's windscreen.

'Not bound to be him, you know, chick,' he said to her. 'Or her. Might be a woman. There may be several people in the house. No telling. Don't jump to conclusions. It is usually patient good police work that gets results.'

Jenny was sitting at her desk with a pile of files in front of her. She had been allowed to leave or delegate her other work in order to get on with the search for someone with whom she had recently come into contact, someone who bore her a grudge. Her eyes were still red. Her face looked small, miserable.

'I ain't done nuthin' to nobody,' she said quietly, trying to make a joke of it.

'Keep on looking.'

It was the following morning when she came to Dave with a folder.

'I can't believe this is the man,' she said. 'It was so trivial. Surely no one in their right mind would think twice about it.'

'What? What are you drivelling on about, woman?' teased Dave.

Silently she handed him the papers from the folder.

'A traffic offence?' he said incredulously. 'You're a detective, not a bloody traffic warden. What is all this?'

'It could have been a fatal accident. The driver was well over the speed limit on a road with children crossing after school. About half-past three. He only just slowed down in time. One little girl was nearly knocked over. Fortunately she was only badly shaken, but she could easily have been killed. Two little boys were running out of the school gates. One couldn't stop running, the car was still moving, the boy landed on the bonnet of the car.'

'So how were you involved, and what makes you say it was trivial? It sounds very serious indeed to me.'

'Potentially very serious. The driver said the children had dashed in front of the car. There wasn't a lollipop lady on duty for some reason so his claim couldn't be refuted, not for sure. I was walking home. My day off and I'd been shopping. I was quite close. He looked as though he would drive off. I ran forward, leaned on his open window, and gave him an earful. Also took his number and asked to see his licence.'

'And?'

'He asked who the hell I thought I was, pushing my long nose into what didn't concern me. I said I was an off-duty police officer. Oh, goodness.'

'What?'

'He demanded to know my name and I gave it. Detective Constable Wren.'

In the university, later that day, Angela went for the first time to the Women's Group with Jess. The room was small; out of all the women students in the university few seemed concerned enough to come. Angela looked round and decided that these were the activists, the live wires who put their time and energy into the cause. The attacks in the city surely raised consciousness more than this?

It was a good meeting and she was glad she had attended.

'Will you come again?' asked Jess as they walked back to their hall of residence.

'Yes, I will,' said Angela.

'I'm glad.' Jess felt that they had definitely become friends. 'You're bound to have lots of social life, it would be easy for you not to bother.'

'Lots of social life?'

'Lots of the men will ask you out, or want to involve you in other societies.'

'I think the Women's Group is something I will want to keep on, whatever happens. Listening to the discussion tonight made me realise the fight for equality hasn't yet been won. I thought it had. I'm not sure about the "lots of men" bit either, Jess. The whole sex thing seems to me to be a minefield. How many married couples are happy? Strange things happen. People have peculiar attitudes.'

'I suppose so,' Jess said vaguely.

'Sometimes I wish I'd studied psychology or social studies.'

'Surely you don't!'

'Well, perhaps it is only a passing fancy. But women novelists of the nineteenth century can seem irrelevant to life today.'

'Oh but ...' began Jess, and the argument which started then went on until they parted at midnight. After they reached their floor, Jess suggested they went on talking over a hot drink on the landing. Once there, they were joined by a crowd of other girls, mostly in daytime clothes but some of them in pyjamas or dressing-gowns. If they weren't reading English, at least they all had opinions about the syllabus and its relevance, and the discussion grew quite heated. Women's issues came into it. At first Angela said less than anyone, but she thoroughly enjoyed herself. Looking over at her, at the chin resting on the hand, at the falling curtain of blonde hair, at the long legs twisted round the legs of a stool as she argued or listened totally unselfconsciously, Jess felt a glow of pleasure. She was a friendly soul, and to have Angela as one of the planets revolving in her sky made her feel enriched. No one knew how the discussion worked itself round to sex and the attacker.

'The police say,' quoted a girl in black satin pyjamas, 'that women should reduce the risk of being attacked by not wearing provocative clothing, but sticking to comfortable shoes and clothes, so that they can move easily. Also that they should keep their hands out of their pockets, and avoid wearing personal stereos. It's in a booklet.'

'You don't want to believe all you read,' said Jess 'The police never talk about provocative clothing, haven't you noticed that? It is always the defence barristers or sometimes the judges who use those words.'

'It says we should consider the effect our clothes might have on others,' went on the girl in black satin. 'And face oncoming traffic, stay in the middle of the pavement out of reach of bushes, and keep in well-lit areas.'

'Ever been grabbed by a bush?' giggled someone.

'Have you got the booklet? Let's have a

look at it,' said Angela. The girl in black pyjamas passed it over.

A tall girl called Mercy, reading over Angela's shoulder, said, 'This is reducing women to second-class citizens. Any woman should be able to walk through the city without being molested, no matter what she is wearing.'

'In theory you are right,' said Angela, 'but better safe than sorry.'

Mercy seemed unreasonably incensed by this, and repeated herself, with variations. 'Of course I'm right. Even if a woman chose to walk naked she ought to be safe. It is every woman's right to walk where she wants to, wear what she wants to, when she wants to, talk to anyone she wants to and go anywhere she wants to. The first thing the police say of an attack—well, all right, Jess, not the police, who are very circumspect—the thing the newspapers say, and the defence barristers, I'm sure you're right, Jess—' sarcastically—'is bound to be that the woman's clothing was provocative.'

'It is a matter of common sense,' argued

Angela. 'Anyway, if anyone walked round in public naked they'd get arrested, and surely they'd be asking for trouble.'

Several girls cried out in denial of this. 'It should make no difference what anyone wears,' they said more or less in chorus.

Angela, who was still in her running gear, noticed that she was covered up less than any of the others. Apart from a couple of girls wearing long dresses down to the ankle over their clumpy shoes, everyone not in very modest nightwear wore trousers in black or very dark blue, with long-sleeved tops down to the wrist and up to the throat. She didn't think this was compatible with the views they were expressing.

'You must admit none of you is dressed provocatively,' she said.

'Well, no. We don't dress to attract men. We despise all that.'

Angela felt helpless in this argument. 'But you say it shouldn't make any difference what women wear, then imply that men are very much affected by women's clothing,' she said.

It was only when other students appeared from their rooms, complaining that they couldn't sleep for the noise, that the group broke up.

Angela was unhappily conscious that she seemed to have made an enemy of Mercy, who had ignored her parting 'Goodnight,' in a very pointed way. She regards me as a traitor to my sex, Angela thought. But I think the police are right. They may go a bit far, with this sitting downstairs on a bus, near the driver—how do they know the driver is safe, if things are that dangerous?—but I go along with some of it.

The next morning Angela was up early although she had gone to bed so late. She was out running before the mist lifted from the surface of the lake. On her return she paused to go into the college toilets on the ground floor, before climbing the stairs to her room. She happened to choose a cubicle which had been decorated with graffiti. Although she ignored it she could not help noticing one phrase.

A cucumber is better than a man, it read.

As she ran lightly up the stairs a couple of minutes later Angela wondered what disillusion had led to that, what failure in what unknown facet of life. Personally she didn't like cucumber and always left it on the side of her plate. Before showering she looked out of her window. The mist was much thinner, but it was persisting for a long time this morning. She loved the way it obscured hard-edged buildings and lent mystery to the distances.

5

Bob was still in charge of the enquiry. Very little progress was being made in spite of their efforts, but that is the way it is sometimes. After all these weeks, the pattern was still that if the attacker's victims struggled hard enough he ran away.

Until now.

Now, at last, he must have persisted in his blows in spite of the flailing arms, until the girl lay dead. As usual he had cut and torn her clothing, then pulled it up and down to reveal her whole torso to the dim moistness of night. Death had taken place around twelve, but it was only at dawn that she was found.

Two students from the university were out on an early morning jog through the mist, not round the campus but from their digs in Bootham. They were chatting to each other as they jogged along the quiet paths and alleyways of the inner city suburb. Turning at last on to a tarmac path alongside grass, separated by black railings from the railway track to Scarborough, they saw dimly through the damp haze a pale shape on the grass ahead. The shape did not move. They jogged towards it, thinking it looked like a human being lying there on the grass.

'Homeless,' gasped one of them, a lad called Shane. 'Sleeping rough.'

'Too cold,' gasped the other lad, Jason. 'Need shelter.' Breathing heavily, 'Doorway. Cardboard box.'

There was no time for more speculation. Their swift steps had taken them up to the shape and they stopped short.

The shape was that of a young woman, hardly looking more than a teenager, her clothing wrenched from her thin body. The head was tilted oddly to one side and a trickle of blood had dried on her cheek, running down from behind her ear.

The two young male students were never to forget that moment.

'This is awful,' said Jason in a whisper.

'I think she's dead.'

'Looks like,' whispered Shane.

'What do we do?' Jason was looking queasy.

'Find a phone, get help,' Shane said softly. 'I'll stay here.' I don't think Jason could stand guarding her, he thought, he looks really rough.

Jason ran off, and began to knock on doors. He saw a light in one window and his urgent banging brought a frowsty, half-asleep man in his forties to answer him.

'Can I phone the police, please, it's urgent ...' Or ought I to ring an ambulance first? he wondered. Both, why not. He stumbled after the man into the hallway of the Edwardian terrace house and picked up the phone. The man stood by, curious.

'Police, fire or ambulance?' asked the girl.

'Police, please, then, ambulance ... Oh hello, my name is Jason Black. I am phoning from number thirty-five Sycamore Street, Bootham. There's a girl on the side of the path near the railway track, she looks dead.'

Jason stopped to take breath and the man, who had listened in astonishment, pulled on a jacket and went out of the front door to see what was happening.

'Your mate's phoning from my house,' he said to Shane when he arrived at the scene. 'Don't you think you ought to give her the kiss of life?' He stared down at the nude body of the girl.

'She's dead,' said Shane. 'Cold. No pulse. Not breathing.'

'You might have saved her with the kiss of life,' said the man.

'Leave her alone,' said Shane bitterly. 'Don't disturb the evidence or you'll be for it.'

Within minutes the first police officer was on the scene, bringing with him a portable tent to put over the body. He wrote down the names and addresses of the two students and the man from the terrace house, thanked them for being so public-spirited and suggested politely that there was nothing else they could do, thank you very much.

Shane and Jason exchanged a long look.

They were very shaken and not sure what to do with themselves. How could they just jog off to the uni after this?

'I suppose we'd better go,' Shane said at last. 'All right?'

'Of course,' said Jason, white-faced.

Shane said nothing else, but they turned with one accord and, slowly at first, began to jog again. They didn't speak until they reached the campus.

'Scary, eh?' said Shane.

'You're not kidding.'

The first police officer on the scene started a log of times and names of those present. He was to continue this with all departures and arrivals throughout the morning. When the next police officer appeared—a man senior in the force to himself—the two together put up tape round the perimeter of the area and left only one entrance, a passageway through to the body. The man from Sycamore Street went away, disappointed, to prepare for work. The two students had already left.

Bob Southwell was contacted and, jerked

fully awake by the news, telephoned Bruno Hallam within minutes.

'I'll be down,' said Hallam, 'but you know what to do, Bob. You've been in charge so far. Carry on as if I didn't exist, but I will be down later to have a recce.'

When Bob, hastily dressed, arrived by the railway track the doctor had already pronounced life extinct. He earned his money pretty easily, the policemen believed; he himself thought that for turning out at ungodly hours he deserved every penny. Screens and the tent now protected the body and prevented the public from catching any glimpse. The whole familiar team was clustered round. The ground nearby had already been examined and was protected from further damage. The photographer was busy taking videofilm and still shots of the pathetic corpse, the thin ribcage collapsed, the flat non-sexy breasts which now would never ripen, the childlike stomach and thin hips, the flat Mount of Venus scantily covered with mousy hair. The girl's face was thin too, the hair on her head also mousily fair.

Her expression was faintly surprised. There was little blood. Her bag—a largish affair of black plastic which was a cross between a hold-all and a handbag—lay at her side.

Bob Southwell was standing looking down at the body from a couple of yards away, when a black official police car came up. Bruno Hallam was the first to emerge. James Jester, a young detective constable, was one of the others who got out of the car afterwards.

'How is progress?' Hallam asked South-well when he reached him.

'Very routine at present.'

'Put me in the picture.'

'Age about twenty. We have already found out quite a lot about her from her handbag, which also put us on to her friends. Her name is Ann Clark. She worked in the typing pool of a local firm. Not married. Worked late on overtime last night. We assume she was walking home, it was her normal route, apparently. Lives near here in a house shared with four other girls. We are still checking her background.'

'Not raped, by the look of it,' said Hallam.

'Doesn't look like it. We'll know soon enough. The coroner has been informed, and the post-mortem is set up for this afternoon.'

'Not possible for this morning?'

'No, sir. One o'clock was the earliest we could arrange it.'

'I will keep a watching brief on this, Bob. I would like to be in touch at all times and informed of progress and events on a regular basis. But I leave the conduct of the investigation to you. Unless, of course, reasons arise to make my involvement necessary. Did you contact the offender-profiling people? I remember you were intending to do that a while ago.'

'They have arranged to start this week.'

'Good. Tell them we would like their input as soon as possible. Obviously it can only supplement normal methods but the more aspects of the enquiry are working together the better. Having killed, he's likely to go on to worse and worse orgies.'

Hallam stood for a while in silence, then

without further word turned and left the scene.

So that's it, thought Bob. The limit of his involvement? I doubt it, on reflection. He'll be wanting to stick his oar in. Inevitably. And subconsciously Bob Southwell knew that he was not sorry to have Hallam in place. Detective Superintendent Duncan had been a strong boss who had moved on to higher things. Detective Superintendent Birch, who had succeeded him, was a popular man whose declining health over the last few years had prevented him from being the can-carrier and buck-stopper that a DCI has the right to expect in his superior officer. There had often been times when Bob had wished for a stronger head of division, though his personal loyalty to Birch had never faltered. Now he was meeting a new situation. Although he had to struggle to feel personal liking for Hallam—and had still not managed it—there was no doubt that the new super had earned respect. He had shown himself to be outstandingly efficient, reliable and sensitive to the needs of his staff. What was still to be seen was how he would react to the difficulties of a murder enquiry. By leaving it to me? wondered Bob Southwell.

Southwell remembered the time when he first came to York—before his first murder case. The murder had happened during a rehearsal of the medieval Mystery Plays. He had not realised then, himself, the character of this lowland city to which he had so lightly moved his family from Harrogate.

So many York inhabitants had been born in York, and their families before them. They had worked in the same two industries, father to son, mother to daughter. They had walked the same streets, shopped in shops on the same ground that their grandparents had walked and shopped on before them. Inward-looking, they were content to be parochial, as such communities are. People like himself, the incomers, were as different as chalk from cheese, with different preoccupations. He knew that Bruno Hallam was unlikely, yet, to realise how close a community he was dealing with.

It was the first proper murder in York for some time—proper in the sense of needing this kind of investigation. There had been murders, yes, since the killing at Barley Hall and the shooting in Bishophill, but they had been of the normal run. Two wives had been murdered by their husbands, and one husband had been murdered by his wife. The guilty people had immediately confessed. A pub brawl had resulted in a fatal stabbing. But all that had been obvious; obvious motives, obvious killers, obvious, predictable trials and sentences to come. The hunt for this assailant was something else again.

'We knew he would murder sooner or later,' Dave Smart had said. They had expected it. The question was, had murder been the attacker's object? Once he had progressed—or descended—to this level, would its excitement be heady enough—irresistible enough—to keep him at it? Or was it only a blip in his career? Whichever, they could take no chances.

Bob came back from his thoughts, and

was intensely aware once more of the scene around him. Ahead, the line of iron railings which bordered the path, their black paint flaking, revealing traces of the rust beneath; then long grass of fading green and the grey-brown river beyond. The farther bank was still hidden by mist. Here, in the damp morning, this sad frail body of a girl.

Then he became aware of the young policeman standing at his elbow.

'James,' he said. 'Forgotten you'd arrived, for a minute. I would like you to take over as exhibits officer on this case. You have done the job before, so I don't need to explain.'

'I understood that was why you wanted me, sir. I have brought the bags and bottles.'

The bags were for clothing and similar things, such as the handbag, the bottles for blood and other samples, and swabs. They would go to the lab at Wetherby, if the senior officer, Bob in this case, and the forensic scientist from the Wetherby laboratory decided they should. At one time, James remembered, the whole lot would have been packed off to Wetherby; but now that every item had to be paid for it was different. The lab having become a separate business, the decision-making process involving Bob and the forensic bloke had been added to the procedure. James was fairly sure that in this case everything would be sent. He set about his task of bagging up and giving each item an identifying code.

The forensic scientist was already on his way from Wetherby, and the forensic pathologist was on his way from Sheffield. The likelihood was that the Wetherby man would arrive first because he had a shorter journey, but as the pathologist had a sports car and drove like a bat out of hell, they might well arrive at the same time. James Jester looked forward to seeing them at work. He liked the way they stood still, gazing for a while, sizing up the situation, knowing each other so well that grunts and murmurs were enough to convey thoughts. Then they would move in for their closer examinations. And all the time he himself, as exhibits officer, would be there whenever required, part of the process.

The young woman looked even more pathetic on the slab at the post-mortem that afternoon. A forensic pathologist at work was a sight Bob Southwell would rather not watch, but this man was a personal friend, and even in these circumstances Bob could admire his skill, whether wielding saw or scalpel.

The steady drone of comment went on into the recording machine. As the examination moved through its routine, Bob stiffened in surprise. The girl was a virgin, and untouched. No rape. The blows which killed her were inflicted by something which might be a cosh of some kind, not as lethal as a hammer. The blows would not have killed a normal person, a strong, well-nourished girl.

'Would you mind repeating that?' asked Bob.

The pathologist looked up in annoyance.

'Don't interrupt,' he said. 'It's all on the tape, and in my notes, and will be in the report.'

They were good friends but at this rebuke Bob fell silent. Then, before going on, the pathologist said, repeating his earlier words but this time rather sternly directing them at Bob. 'This girl's skull is abnormally thin. The word "eggshell" comes to mind.' He dropped his head again and concentrated on his work, his voice resuming its even mutter.

I hope that word doesn't get out, thought Bob Southwell. We will have to carefully paraphrase it, or better still avoid mentioning the thinness of the skull. It must not in any circumstances be mentioned. Otherwise ...! Otherwise he could visualise what kind of newspaper headlines there might be.

'Murder victim had eggshell thin skull.' No, they wouldn't be so verbose. Perhaps 'Eggshell Killer'. And what was the significance? Great. This man, all right, or woman, might or might not have meant to kill. Whether it was intentional or not, the thinness of the skull might suggest an argument for manslaughter. How would he/she react now they had killed? Why bother thinking 'she'—all the victims who could give a description had said it was a man ...

As usual, the pathologist and Bob Southwell went off for a drink and a sandwich before the pathologist set off for home. They went to a city-centre pub, and the pathologist had half a pint and a chicken sandwich. They hadn't been there five minutes when Brian, the forensic scientist, came in and spotted them in a dark corner.

'I had a sort of feeling you two might still be about,' he said. 'Can I join you?'

'How many pubs have you been in, looking for us?' Bob asked tartly.

'This is the first. Honest. I saw you walk in as I was looking for somewhere to park the car. My afternoon off. Helping the wife with a bit of shopping.'

'Go and help her, then,' said the pathologist.

'I'd rather talk to you two. Tell me about the PM.'

'The girl's skull was thinner than usual, that fact is agitating our boy in blue here.'

Bob said nothing.

'Also she was an untouched virgin. Surprised?' the pathologist asked.

'Very.' Brian lost his cheerful look. 'I'll join you in half a pint.'

Bob had treated himself to a beef sandwich. He had added rather too much mustard. What with mustard, beef and bread, not to mention the garnish of salad, his voice was indistinct.

'I can't understand his motives,' Bob went on after a few seconds and a swig of bitter. 'If he doesn't want to rape or rob—nothing has been taken as far as we can tell, in any of the cases, not even clothing—why go around hitting people on the head with coshes?'

'Not likely to be a proper cosh, in my opinion,' said Brian, the forensic scientist, judicially. 'Don't you agree, Edward?' He had turned to the pathologist.

'We have had discussions about that in the force,' interposed Bob Southwell when it was obvious the pathologist was not going to contribute anything on that point. 'A sock full of Scarborough sand seems to be the usual theory. The weighted hosepipe has lost credence. Old-fashioned, we feel.'

'Fashion in murder weapons! There's an interesting subject for someone to write a thesis about,' said the pathologist.

'Why pull the clothes up and down unless he wants to touch or desecrate?' asked Bob.

'Looking is enough, perhaps,' said Brian.

'No, there is something else behind it.'

'How is the enquiry going?'

'Full-scale incident room set up this morning. The HOLMES program has been started on the computer. We're carrying out all the normal procedures. As it happens, we had already called in the offender-profiling people. One of our detective constables went on a course. Might save us time, which is money. It is another arrow in the armoury. Not an exact science. Of course, for some time we've been looking carefully at all the preceding incidents.'

'Naturally.'

The next item on Bob Southwell's programme was the media conference, fixed for four o'clock. There had been a discussion about exactly how much to reveal, which details were to be kept secret. This was vital in order to weed out the false confessions which were bound to come in. The police can do without the attention seekers. There has to be some method of sorting them out from the real murderer. Also it was important to maintain interest in the case; information from the public sometimes needed coaxing out over a period of days or weeks, so not all the details would be given at once.

Hallam turned up for the media conference, but sat quietly without intervening. Bob glossed over the facts he did not want to emphasise. This was in many ways a low-key murder; its main significance was its place in the series of attacks. Consequently he was able to control media reaction well.

It was usual during the first days of a murder enquiry for the police to work steadily all the hours there were, but today

Bob thought his team were working well enough to spare him briefly, so he slipped home for an hour to eat the evening meal. As usual the children, bathed and in their pyjamas, were sitting on the white Flokati rug in front of the television watching a video, together with Pease-blossom the young Siamese cat, who didn't much like the programme and was thinking of going to sleep. But as soon as Bob went into the room Paul and Susan jumped up and ran to him, upsetting Pease-blossom, who had been stretched across Susan's knee with one paw on Paul.

'Daddy! Daddy! We heard at school that somebody killed somebody!' Paul said.

'Bop on the head,' said Susan, bopping her brother, who shook her off impatiently.

'Killed dead,' added Paul.

How on earth had the news got round so quickly? Local radio, of course. Bob remembered being told that there had been a news item on at one o'clock. He answered his son gravely.

'Yes, I'm afraid someone did kill somebody.'

'You know all about it, Daddy?' said Paul, questioning.

'I've been working on it all day, and as soon as I've eaten that lovely meal your mother's serving out I'm going back to work on it some more. Won't be home again until long after you two are asleep in bed, so how about a cuddle now?'

'We're going to take Pease-blossom to bed, Daddy. Mummy says we've been good and we can take her upstairs, and I'm to have her first,' said Susan, snuggling into one of his circling arms as her brother claimed the other.

'Daddy! Daddy!' said Paul. 'Do you know who killed that poor lady?'

'We're going to find out.'

The killer had chosen his victim singularly well, if he had intended to kill her—but it was on the cards that he had not intended the consequences of his act. Unconsciousness had apparently been his aim in earlier attacks.

The girl had begun life as a thin, undernourished baby who was abandoned in a telephone kiosk. No one ever knew her real name. She was called after Ann Clark, the eleven-year-old who found her and acted in a very responsible way, saving the baby's life by wrapping it in her own jacket and cuddling it to the warmth of her body. The baby had grown up in care to be a thin, undernourished, unloved child and, finally, young woman. She had few possessions, but her one known talent kept her in reasonable funds. She was an expert copy typist. Any document could be placed in front of her and she could type it into the computer at an extremely fast and yet accurate rate. Since her office had bought an expensive state-of-the-art scanner it might have been thought that she would become redundant, but there were enough documents the scanner couldn't handle to keep her very busy. If a document had a blot on it they said she would copy-type the blot, but that judgement should properly have been made about the scanner.

Her friends in the office tried to include her in their social life. She went along and seemed grateful, but never reciprocated and seemed just as happy when left alone. So it was that while all over the city young women were making careful arrangements to be escorted home, she slipped off quietly on her own on foot and took the lonely path towards the shared house.

The news spread over the city as the ripples on a pond spread over the surface. Someone knew someone who heard it on local radio or whose milkman had passed the end of the street just as the police drove up. Students who lodged near the scene of the incident, walking innocently along the path on their way to the university bus, were stopped and made to take another route by a uniformed policeman, but Shane and Jason had not been asked to keep quiet about their experience so they told their friends.

The news ran from one department to another across the campus. Angela heard it about one o'clock as she left the college restaurant and headed across the bridge to the Morrell Library for the afternoon. The way it was told her, with all the emphasis on horror, made her cling to a handrail and she was dizzy for a second. The look of gloating fascination on the face of the fellow student, a man she hardly knew, made her feel ill. She hid her distress and managed to appear politely interested, but once at a table in the library she found herself thinking about the murder when she should have been taking notes.

As well as the map with its coloured pins, and all the other diagrams, photos and data sheets, Bob Southwell had a calendar on the wall of the room which had, in the space of half an hour that morning, become an incident room. Sandra, one of the part-time staff, had photocopied the individual sheets and pinned them up for him all along one side of the room. On these sheets the dates of the attacks had been recorded. The detectives spent a lot of time standing in front of this and thinking about the time sequence. It seemed to them that the patterns on map and calendar and various charts had

119

significance if they could only crack the code.

'It is not that simple,' said James Jester, the only officer in the station who had been on the offender-profiling course. 'Criminal spatial behaviour from solved crimes,' he explained straight from his memory of his course notes, 'is used to test the predictive accuracy of geographical and psychological methods of establishing an offender's home base from crime scene locations.'

'All right, James,' said DCI Southwell, 'get cracking, then. Co-operate with these blokes that are coming to help us with this. Though we are more likely to solve it by what we are doing already.'

'Perhaps he's a lunatic and only bashes people on the head at the full of the moon,' suggested the office wag.

'Right,' said Bob Southwell. 'Your job, Mark, find a lunar calendar and check your theory out.'

'That'll keep him quiet for five minutes,' said Dave Smart.

'More than five with any luck, and James might come up with something.

The money we spent on his course should give a return at last. Soon we will know how old the murderer was, when he lost his mother and whether he wears green socks.'

The forensic examination which took place a while later at Wetherby was intense, but the fibres and other minute pieces of evidence on the clothing showed no unusual features—nothing distinctive enough to be a clue.

They are all the same, you see. That's what people don't seem to understand. It's got to be demonstrated by taking their clothes off. Then everyone can see they are all the same underneath. It doesn't matter if they are young or old, it is still Eve and the Serpent. Eve was created to help Adam but she only tempted him to grossness.

That little one, she was too thin to show it properly. But at least she was saved from becoming like the others, she can thank me for that.

The police force burnt the midnight oil

over little Ann Clark. After that brief visit home, Bob was up all night with the rest, directing the team. But her murderer was as far from the clutches of the law as he had been before that abnormally thin skull had caved in surprisingly under his cosh—so easy to hide, so useful for the job in hand.

Later in the week, exhausted after several days of round the clock work with hardly any sleep, Bob decided a short break was essential. He slept like the dead for several hours, and on waking realised that it was seven in the evening and a Thursday, the one night when he usually went to the pub with Tom Churchyard from next door.

'I'll pop in and see old Tom on my way back to the station,' he said to Linda as he knotted his tie.

'One pint, and that's it, Tom,' he said a few minutes later in the Grey Mare.

'It sounds awful to say this,' Bob said quietly to Tom when they had settled with their pints in a corner, 'but we won't catch him until he kills again. If then.'

'You do sound pessimistic.'

'You can say that again.'

'You do sound pessimistic,' complied Tom.

'Idiot. Perhaps this pint will make me less pessimistic.'

'I hope so. It is Thursday, after all. The night you are usually able to get away from everything.'

There was no getting away that wintry night. Half an hour was all Bob allowed himself. As he walked wearily back to the incident room the lamplight in the wet streets showed them empty, forsaken. When women went abroad in their own locality they did so in twos, and fearfully. Behind their curtains they talked over the poor girl's death. Even if their minds went briefly off the subject—a general election might be taking place, a civil war in some far-off country, a particularly bad accident on the M25, the only bittern in England booming its last—the people of York, no longer only the women, were not to be diverted for long from the real issues.

At the university they were having another Women's Group meeting, and this time it was not simply a few activists in a small room. They had booked the Lyons Concert Hall and the student body had turned up *en masse*. There was hardly a spare seat.

6

Julia Brandsby, whose friend Linda Southwell called her Julie on the analogy of
Charles to Charlie, Elizabeth to Lizzie
and Rebecca to Becky, was walking down
Stonegate, one of the oldest streets in
the city, when she saw Tom Churchyard
coming towards her. Julia had already
been that morning to the self-defence
for women class in Moss Street. She
was feeling heated and exhilarated after
the exercise, but a little tired. Now, with
the low wintry sun lighting up the pale
stone of the Minster ahead of her so that
the ancient building glowed, she had to go
and run into Tom.

It was some time since the two of them
had met. In fact the last occasion was at
a dinner party at the Southwells' house.
Tom was a bachelor, a British Telecom
engineer, who lived next door to Julia's

friends, in the other semi of the pair of semi-detached houses. He got to know the Southwells when they moved to York from Harrogate and was particularly friendly with Bob. Julia was mainly friendly with Linda. Neither Bob nor Linda knew that Julia and Tom had had an affair.

The question for Julia was, had Tom seen her? Would he see her? If he didn't, could she pass him without speaking, pretending not to notice him? That would be much the simplest, she would prefer that. But if he did see her, what then?

Stonegate is a narrow street, often crowded with tourists. It is easy not to notice people. It would be hard to notice everyone. Tom, however, had seen Julia the minute he entered the street from the Minster end. For him her slim figure in a lightweight grey coat, a white blouse just showing at the neck, with her black hair swinging forward on to both cheeks in twin smooth curves, her air of neatness and elegance, stood out from the crowd like a good deed in a naughty world. His heart missed a beat, he was sure. It felt as though it had. His breathing was constricted. He was conscious of every yard they travelled towards each other, although he did not look directly at her.

It was their second meeting since the end of their love affair.

The first had been at that dinner party, which had been very difficult for both of them. After the high drama, the self-sacrifice, of their parting, they had met unexpectedly that evening and, without notice, had to appear to be casual acquaintances. Every moment conscious of the other's presence, they had almost ignored one another and made polite conversation with the other guests.

Now they were walking along Stonegate towards one another. Stonegate was busy, mainly with tourists carrying cameras. The architecture of the ancient buildings is interesting, particularly if passers-by lift their eyes above the shops to the façades above, to see all the variety of styles and periods.

Tom and Julia simultaneously decided to acknowledge each other. Tom got ready a polite word of greeting and Julia prepared a pleasant, friendly but non-committal smile.

'Hi! Not a bad sort of day,' said Tom.

'Much better weather,' said Julia. 'That mist has lifted, thank goodness.'

'Season of mists and mellow frightfulness,' misquoted Tom.

They stood still and neither was willing to be the first to move on.

'Care for a coffee?' asked Tom, rather hesitant. 'I can take a ten-minute break. My second-in-command is on site.'

As usual in Tom's life, an important excavation for a large junction box was taking place in one of the city streets, creating as little nuisance as possible, which in crowded York city centre meant a great deal of nuisance.

'Why not?' said Julia.

There were many reasons why not, and the fact that since the dinner party she had been going out regularly with Richard Sugden, whom she had met that evening, was not the least of them.

There were teashops in the street but by

mutual consent they headed for the nearest pub, which had fallen in with the modern trend and served coffee and food as well as everything else. Tom could not drink during his working hours, Julia was longing for a hearty shot of caffeine, and they had frequented this pub before. It was down an alleyway. The very place, as it happened, where they had once lunched together and overheard a conversation which was very important to the police. Remembering that time, Julia looked around nervously as they entered, but she could see no one resembling a terrorist. She breathed again. She had had enough of that kind of excitement to last a lifetime.

There was a pause as they ordered a coffee and a scone each. They were weighing each other up, noticing the small changes and the things which remained the same. Julia wore her inevitable black shoes and black tights, with clothing in her favourite colours of grey and white. Tom, a large man with big features which would in time look distinguished, was in his working clothes, casual trousers and a jumper under an oldish jacket of hairy tweed. They both looked slightly older.

'Still seeing Sugden?' Tom asked at last.

'Yes.'

Tom didn't say anything else for a while.

'Are you seeing anyone?' asked Julia.

'Not at the moment.'

Tom left that sentence in the air, hoping that it implied he had been seeing loads of glamorous women and intended to see many more as soon as he got round to it. The fact was (as Julia knew very well) that this big, efficient, tweedy man, still in his mid-thirties, was shy and reserved and apart from Julia there had been no one in his romantic life since a rebuttal many years ago which had hurt him profoundly.

The coffee and scones arrived.

'How is Adam?' asked Tom politely.

Adam was Julia's son. Her husband had died many years before. It was partly Adam's possessiveness of his mother which had spoilt their romance, though there had been plenty of other factors.

130

'He's well. Away now at university. St Andrews.'

'Oh,' said Tom, and they were both silent for a while.

'Isn't it awful about this murder,' they both began to say at the same time, stopped, smiled.

'It's not funny,' Julia said sternly as if the smile was all Tom's fault.

'We can hardly be surprised after all the incidents there have been. Didn't you expect it?'

'Everyone has been expecting a murder, but that doesn't make it any less horrific now it's happened.'

'You don't go out on your own at night, do you, Julia?' asked Tom anxiously.

'Of course not. I'm not daft.'

There was a long pause. Fortunately they both had some coffee and scone left to occupy them.

'I'm glad I saw you,' Tom said at last, 'because I got something through the post this morning which will interest you.'

He fished out a piece of paper from his pocket and passed it to Julia It was an

131

announcement of an exhibition to be held in one of the colleges of York University.

'Dolls and dolls' houses,' Julia read aloud. 'Why did you think it would interest me, Tom?'

'Crafts,' he replied. 'You are interested in all textile crafts, and dolls are mostly textile, aren't they? And dolls' houses are full of bits of textile? I looked at it and thought, this would be right up Julia's street, and put it in my pocket. It is a coincidence that I saw you.'

'Yes.' Julia was thoughtful. 'If you believe in coincidence.' The illustration on the handbill was intriguing. 'What would have happened if you hadn't seen me, which was much more likely?'

'I was going to give it to Linda and ask her to pass it on.'

'Why were you sent one, anyway?'

'As chairman of the Medieval Reconstruction Society I get all sorts of odd things through the post.'

Julia put the handbill away in her bag and forgot it.

They talked of other things, and, once

outside in the street again, parted with a slight regret. Tom turned after a few yards to look back at her and found that she had turned to look back at him. She lifted her hand in a tiny gesture of farewell and he waved back. They both hesitated, then turned once more and went on their separate ways.

Julia thought about Tom and their meeting a good deal during the next few days. She had found a dear friend and lover in Richard Sugden, the Chief Constable who had come to spend his retirement in York. Even to have had a cup of coffee with Tom seemed disloyal. If Tom had also found someone else, she could have put him out of her mind for ever. To know that he had a lingering love for her made her uncomfortable, but after a while she decided it was common sense to try to forget him.

It was when she ate her lunch in the King's Manor Refectory a few days later that the exhibition at the university came to her attention again. King's Manor, in the centre of the city of York, is a lovely conglomeration of different periods and styles of building which, having been used for many different purposes during its lifetime, is now an outflung part of the University of York, whose main campus is at Heslington. The public can eat in the refectory and enjoy the atmosphere, and many of them do. On leaving in the autumn they pass the golden glory of the tree which annually gives the Midas touch to the pale stone, creamy gravel and leaded windows of the first of the two quadrangles. Julia loved this tree. After admiring it, she stood for a while in the deep archway which joined the two open spaces, reading the notices on the board there. So much was always going on in the university! Story-telling evening. Folksong events. Various specialised types of music, the gamelan, or church music on original instruments. An exhibition of dolls and dolls' houses.

Wait a minute. There was something ... She began to root in her shoulder bag. The leaflet Tom had given her that day they met in Stonegate. She found it crushed in the bottom under her purse, wallet, comb, diary, cheque book and handkerchief. Unfolding the creased-up thing she compared it with the more showy and colourful poster on the board. The more she thought about it, the more Julia, who was a textile expert and designer of embroideries, was surprised, charmed, intrigued. The private view had been the night before. It was open to the public that very day, if she wanted to see it. She did. She had nothing pressing to do, so she would go now, immediately, forthwith.

It was not like the university to have an exhibition of dolls and dolls' houses. Teddy bears, maybe. The staff had a sneaking suspicion that a number of undergraduates had come from home complete with teddy bear. There was something of a social cachet about teddy bears. Some people even went so far as to collect them. But dolls and dolls' houses?

On the other hand, no one had seen dolls or dolls' houses like these before. They had all been handmade by craftsmen and craftswomen, each as individual as a thumbprint, the sort of thing which in a hundred years' time would have the experts on the Antiques Road Show cooing, if the programme, if telly, if civilisation, lasts that long.

Finding a phone box, Julia rang Linda Southwell to ask her if she would like to go too.

'I'd love to, Julie,' said Linda, 'but I can't, today. You must go. It's just up your street.'

Julia made most of her living conserving old fabrics, writing articles on her subject, and designing modern craftwork. 'Just up your street' seemed to be the correct phrase.

'I'll come and fetch you, Linda,' said Julia, who had recently acquired a second-hand car she was afraid of and so far had hardly used. It did have the advantage over her beloved moped of enabling her to offer lifts to friends.

'Not this week—I've too much on. I might manage it at the weekend, and take Susan,' replied Linda.

Julia drove to Heslington and arrived

at the university without a problem. The exhibition was not easy to find. The colleges were signposted on University Road, but once off the road and parked Julia wasn't sure which one was Langwith and which was Vanbrugh. Looking round she admired the place and was glad to be in it, as she usually felt. A handsome man was walking into the car-park. She decided to ask him to direct her; he looked as though he might be a lecturer.

'I'm looking for the exhibition, could you tell me which way ...' she said as he approached.

He had a most charming smile. 'Permit me to escort you,' he said. As they turned to walk together he introduced himself. 'Dr Keith Blow,' he said. 'And you are ...?'

'Nothing to do with the university, I'm afraid,' Julia replied. 'I'm a textile specialist.'

'But how fascinating! Do you know Bradford University at all?'

'Not really,' said Julia.

'They have been doing some conservation work on the textiles from the church in Spitalfields. Very beautiful eighteenth-century fabrics. And more recently, I believe, they have been working on some grave-clothes, or shrouds, this time from an excavation in Hull. That cleansing and so on—stabilisation, I suppose—is in collaboration with our archaeology department here in York, who hope to identify the weaves and dyes and so on.'

'I have heard about the Spitalfields fabrics,' said Julia. 'I ought to be more *au fait* with the work done in the archaeological field, particularly here in our own county—it sounds fascinating.'

'Go that way,' said Dr Blow, coming to a stop and waving his hand at a doorway, 'and up the stairs.'

'Thank you, you have been very kind,' said Julia.

Although she had been absorbed in this conversation, Julia had also been taking in the scene around her. A slight disappointment had crept in as she noticed changes in the university. Knowing that there was pressure to increase student numbers and find spaces for boring bourgeois new buildings to accommodate them, she crossed her fingers and hoped that no one would import scratty little rose beds and symmetrical layouts, ruining the elegance which they were apparently not able to appreciate.

She found the porters' lodge with a porter in it. He directed her to the right flight of stairs. After climbing them she trekked past a group of male students who were flopped in front of a television, and almost unexpectedly arrived in the right place, which was not much more than a wide corridor.

She had thought she would be enchanted and she was. The dolls' houses were fabulous. They cost as much as real houses, but some of them had taken a year of a craftsman's life to make. The roof tiles—each one individually cut, individually mounted on the roof—these alone were worth coming several miles to see. The tiny fitments, all to scale, the rows of copper pans exactly graded in size, the minute embroidery on carpets and upholstery—yes, Julia was enraptured.

Mostly the houses were not for sale, but a good few of the dolls bore price labels. There were several students drifting through the exhibition and obviously enjoying the dolls. After a preliminary walk from one end to the other, followed by a more careful scrutiny, Julia decided she must buy something. There was a plump, middle-aged woman in charge of a till.

'I'm spoilt for choice,' Julia said to her, smiling. There was no answering smile.

A tall blonde girl close to Julia smiled instead.

'Have you seen those in the corner?' she asked.

'Which?'

'Let me show you.'

The dolls she spoke of were only two yards from the plump woman's elbow. They were not pretty, like the pierrots, clowns and Victorian misses which most crafts people had made. This was a different enchantment. They were old people, full of character. Their doll faces were lined, wise, merry, thoughtful. Their clothes were tweeds, hand-knitted jumpers and socks, lisle stockings. They wore spectacles, carried walking sticks, used hearing aids, bent towards one another, walked along together, gave one another a helping hand.

The blonde girl had been watching Julia's face.

'They are hard to resist, aren't they?'

'They are people, not dolls, surely.'

The girl laughed, a musical, low-toned, chuckling laugh. 'I feel like that, too.'

'Do you know,' said Julia, 'I think I know the name of the craftswoman who made these. She lived for a while in Cumbria but I think she's gone south now. A shop in Stonegate had some of her work several years ago.'

Julia was irresistibly drawn to two of the dolls in particular, a man and a woman. They must have been married for fifty years, she decided. And they were exactly like her own in-laws, who she hadn't thought of for ages. She stretched out her hand and lightly touched the short, thick tweed skirt the woman wore.

'I wouldn't be taking the ones you fancy,

would I?' she asked the girl, who smiled gently.

'My grant doesn't run to it, unfortunately. Please don't take any notice of me. I love them all. If I were rich I'd buy an armful.'

'I'm not rich but these two are just like an old couple I used to know. Is this your first year at the university? How do you like it?'

'Very well.'

'I've wondered what it was like, being a student here. Is your room comfortable, are the meals okay?'

'Yes to both questions.'

Julia picked up the two dolls she liked so much and took them to the plump woman. Putting them down on the table, next to the till, Julia said to her whimsically, 'I wonder if they will like living with me? Do you think they will?'

The woman gave her a look of utter contempt.

'Dolls don't choose,' she said shortly, and reached out for the money.

A chastened Julia wrote out a cheque as

the two dolls were wrapped up.

As she left the exhibition, she saw the girl again, standing in the TV area as if she was waiting. The young men who had been flopped round the set had gone. When she saw Julia the girl moved towards her, and Julia paused.

'Did you get them?' the girl asked.

'Oh yes! But do I feel small? Smaller than the dolls. Look—are you in a hurry? If you'd care to join me in a cup of tea I need one—I'll unwrap them and we can both look at them properly.'

Somehow Julia felt drawn to this lovely girl, sure there was an affinity between them in spite of the difference in their ages—Julia was in her late thirties, with the big four-oh hovering on the horizon. She didn't often give way to impulses like this, asking complete strangers to drink tea and examine purchases of delight, but this time she wanted to. So did the girl, obviously, for she said, 'I'd like that. My name's Angela.'

'And mine's Julia. Two people with good taste.'

'I heard what she said to you,' Angela said as they walked along. 'The restaurant is up here.'

'Wasn't she scathing? "Dolls don't choose." Not the way to make friends and influence people. Would you like a bun as well? My treat.'

Anyone would have thought we were the same age, Julia reflected later. About ten, for instance. It had been fun. Such a relief from the reports of the recent murder which were filling the local newspapers. Whatever else could they find to say about it? This afternoon she had been able to forget.

The restaurant was almost empty. Lunch was over and all that was available was the cups of tea and buns she had herself suggested. The unwrapping and minute examination of the two dolls was ahead of them, a delicious prospect. They found a corner table and then enjoyed themselves enormously with the grandfather and grandmother dolls, who were definitely older than either of them. They spent an hour together, talking of many things. One thing they did not talk of was the death of Ann Clark.

As they parted, at the top of a flight of concrete stairs which looked positively lethal, Julia gave Angela her card.

'If ever you would like a change of atmosphere, I would love to see you,' she said. 'You might be interested in what I do, as you like craftwork.'

'Everyone should train their hands to be useful,' answered Angela. 'When I see the exquisite products of the eighteenth century, I feel ashamed that we can't match that skill today.'

'What do you do? Apart from studying, I mean.'

'Sport, mostly. I like running, hurdling. I have done embroidery, in fact I usually have a bit of canvas-work on the go. And I do a bit of dressmaking now and then.'

'Do come sometime,' said Julia

'You work at home, I would be interrupting you.'

'It is often very nice to be interrupted. I have some treasures I would love to show you. It's rare for them to really be appreciated—so many people would think them junk. Bits of old costume, embroidery, a few fans, one with mother-of-pearl sticks, it is rather pretty. And grandmother doll and grandfather doll will enjoy your visit.'

They both laughed.

'Dolls can't choose,' Julia went on, 'and can't offer invitations, but I invite you on their behalf. Give me a ring first, in case I'm away from home, it would be dreadful if you had the journey for nothing.'

'I will come with pleasure,' said Angela.

Julia left for home, walking away from the college building with some regret through the grass and trees, noticing how the evenings were drawing in and the air cooling. She had not been so long in the university, but it was almost dark already and she shivered.

Angela by contrast was surprisingly happy. She felt as though she had been touched by a rainbow. Julia was old enough to be her mother, but their childishness that afternoon had been unmixed joy.

7

York has a mild climate and very little snow, perhaps because it lies low and near to sea level. But there is normally a short spat of snow in the weeks leading up to Christmas, if only to remind the citizens that English weather is no tame pussycat and can constantly spring surprises. Students from the eastern hemisphere are often caught napping by sudden cold and have to rush out to buy warm clothes. Even those bred in England who ought to know better can be seen shivering as they come out of the warm colleges into wintry air, then they dash up to their rooms for a sweater, a jacket, or a long scarf.

To Angela, jacket and long scarf draped over the chair behind her, the cold weather was invigorating and the view from every window of the Morrell Library was exciting.

As she sat at a corner table she could hear the sounds from the road behind and below her, yet look out on her left on to a rising slope whitened by snow lying between the tufts of grass. The slope led her eye upwards to the water tower, grandly medieval in effect, reminding her of Clifford's Tower in York centre. Between her and the building and Siward's Howe behind it was an old white horse grazing among the bushes and trees which softened the bleak outline of the tower.

She became absorbed in her work and it was some hours before she looked up again. By then the old horse had wandered off somewhere else, and the air was full of tiny snowflakes, drifting, almost floating, through the still atmosphere.

Angela began to gather her work together. It was time she went to the canteen for lunch. But before leaving the library, she took one last look on to the slope of the hill. In a minute she would be out in the weather. The dappling of snow had almost gone from the grass although minute flakes still drifted downwards. The ground temperature must be above freezing. A crow lifted from the hill, flapped up into the air, and landed again a few yards away. Then all was still.

She always enjoyed walking up or down the library staircase, which bent round in right angles as it went. Some stairs were built without any regard for the human frame and what is comfortable for it and what strains it. They knew in the eighteenth century, thought Angela, who considered the eighteenth to have been the best century so far if one could discount the lack of knowledge of medicine, and this staircase was as comfortable to use as any built in that enlightened period. Then she passed through the turnstile and out through the foyer.

Suddenly as she walked across the bridge towards the college restaurant where she often met Jess, Angela felt a return of the low spirits which had dogged her ever since the murder. She had not been able to drive the tragedy out of her mind for long, ever since it happened, so she was not surprised at the return of gloom. At the time of the murder she had devoured every newspaper article she could find about it, as though they were goblin fruits, both sweet and poisonous. The case obsessed her. The solitary girl, her life so different to Angela's own, became close in spirit. Perhaps they were not so different—she too felt isolated, but her own sorrows and secret griefs seemed trivial compared to those in the life that was lost. Now as the fine snowflakes found out the ways into her jacket, held loosely round her, and a gust of unexpected wind whipped her hair, she thought the elements were mourning.

Jess had already collected her loaded tray of food and begun to eat when Angela joined her.

'You'll get fat,' Angela remarked in a matter-of-fact voice, looking down at her friend. Unloading her own more modestly filled tray on to the other side of the table she added, 'Very fat.'

'Vegetarians don't get fat,' said Jess with her mouth full. Looking up and examining Angela's face she said, 'Oh, no, you aren't getting all miserable again about that poor girl, are you? I'm sure you've got Swedish ancestry. As well as looking Scandinavian, you've inherited that dreadful gloom.'

'Vegetarians do get fat, and one of my grandmothers was Swedish, so you are half right there, Jess.'

Jessica looked up, momentarily interested. 'How romantic, having a Swedish grandmother.'

Angela pulled out a chair and sat down. 'I am a real mongrel,' she said with a smile. 'My Swedish grandmother married a man from Sheffield, Yorkshire through and through and South Yorkshire at that. But both my other grandparents—my father's family—were from Middle Europe.'

'How fascinating.' Jess wasn't fascinated, actually. 'You look pure Swedish.'

'Not many people are pure anything these days.' The serious look came back to Angela's face.

'You are thinking about that girl,' Jess accused her.

'Yes, I am.'

'It doesn't help her, thinking about her all the time.'

151

'I realise. It isn't voluntary. She appears in my mind. Sometimes I think I'm going mad.' Angela said this lightly enough for Jess not to take it seriously.

'The police are doing all they can. We're doing all we can. We've approached the teacher of that self-defence for women class that's running in York and asked her if she will run one up here.'

'Have you heard from her?'

'Not yet.'

It did not come easily to Angela to be open about her innermost thoughts and feelings, but she had by now a real affection for Jess, and trusted her loyalty and lack of tittle-tattle. So Angela said, 'I am getting a bit worried about this preoccupation of mine. You are right, and I'm sure it isn't healthy. Sometimes I think Ann Clark and I are one person.'

'Don't be so daft. You didn't think that while she was alive, why think it now she's dead?'

'What I said wasn't very well phrased. Let's put it like this. She matters to me and should matter to every one of us, as if we ourselves had been lying there.'

'She does matter like that, of course,' said Jess, moving her salad plate to one side and reaching for her dish of pudding. 'For whom the bell tolls and all that. But you are getting morbid. It isn't healthy. Don't.'

Angela tried to put the murdered girl out of her mind, and to chat brightly to her companion. A few people stopped by their table and spoke, and she responded to them, or Jess did, then they moved on. Mercy came by and drew up a chair. They made room for her. She wasn't Angela's favourite person, since the brush they'd had over provocative clothing, but they made conversation. The lunch hour passed, somehow, and the next seminar approached. The trouble was that Angela knew, underneath, that never for an instant had she stopped thinking about the dead girl since that sudden gust of wind on the bridge had taken her by surprise. From recent experience she knew that this mood would last for hours and she would be quite unable to get rid of it until it chose to lift of its own accord. Those people who knew about the way she had been affected were so concerned that she had stopped mentioning it, their clucking over her was too irritating. Even Jess was liable to fuss, though there Angela could give as good as she got without being afraid of affecting their relationship.

'The attacks in the Huntington area seem to have stopped,' Bob Southwell was remarking to his team at the late afternoon briefing meeting. 'None has occurred since the murder, which was in the Bootham area of course. What conclusion can we draw from that?'

He was expecting an answer when the door opened and Hallam came in.

So far the relationship between Bruno Hallam and Bob Southwell had gone remarkably well. They had been at a news conference together earlier that afternoon. This was obviously one of the times when Hallam looked in with a friendly air, and gazed comprehensively around in the way he had which convinced the force that he could see everything at once, like an eagle surveying the ground far below him for a mouse. Occasionally he made some perceptive comment which confirmed the idea that he knew all there was to know.

Bob Southwell winced. He could have done without this heavenly visitation at that moment.

'Don't mind me,' said Bruno.

'What conclusion can we draw from the fact that there have been no more attacks since the murder?' Bob repeated.

'Moved house,' someone said.

'That's pure conjecture, I'm afraid. Do we think he has given his campaign up?'

'Definitely not,' said someone who wanted to shine in front of the super. 'He will never give up.'

Bruno had come because of the latest list from the intelligence office. The staff there constantly kept an eye on reports from other areas. Although it seemed most likely that the murderer was a local man, the possibility of him having moved into the area recently couldn't be overlooked. Unfortunately,

James Jester had accidentally missed his immediate boss, Robert Southwell, off the circulation label. James thought Bob had already seen the list. Bruno also thought Bob had seen it. There were several new items of information on it, the names of men who had left their own areas and might conceivably be in York, men whose crimes had had features in common with the present series; and there was one name of particular import.

Not having seen the latest info, when Hallam asked, 'What action are we taking about Spendlove?' Bob felt like a fool.

'Spendlove?' he asked blankly.

'In today's list from the intelligence office,' Hallam said with a note of impatience in his voice.

Bob had to admit that he had not seen the list.

Hallam did not say any of the obvious things, such as, 'You bloody well ought to have seen it' or 'What are we paying you for?' No, he just went rather pale and looked grim.

'I seem to have missed seeing that list,'

Bob said with what calm he could.

Spendlove was a name well known to everyone there. All the police forces of Britain had been involved in the search for him, some twelve years before. He had been released from prison early in the current year and had last been heard of—as far as Bob knew—settled in north-west Lincolnshire.

'He left Lincolnshire a fortnight ago,' Hallam said, 'and is believed to be moving north, on the tramp. The Lincolnshire border is not that far away—only some fifty miles. He could easily have travelled up from there to commit all of the assaults, but as long as his domicile was there and the police were checking regularly we have not been taking him into consideration, am I right?'

'That is right,' said Bob through stiff lips. If this most dangerous of criminals was now a vagrant he could be anywhere and extraordinarily difficult to catch. 'Unless he does something, though, we can't just apprehend him.'

Hallam said nothing more, but the whole

room was silently seething with thoughts. Spendlove loose in the area meant a chance of violence and viciousness beyond the experience of anyone there, beyond what had been manifest so far in the attacks or the murder. But a recent murder in Leeds came into their memories.

Fortunately Hallam went a few minutes afterwards. Bob concentrated on the organisation of the interviews of possible witnesses and suspects which were taking place. By the time the next day's work was organised it was late, and Bob decided to go home for a break.

That night, for once, when he got home his wife Linda was not immediately aware of his mood. It had been a good day for her—well, except for the clothes-line—and she was feeling bubbly. Susan had been at home for a few days with influenza, but at last she was on the mend. Paul luckily had not caught it. The children were engrossed in their nightly treat of television, watching a favourite video Paul had been given for his birthday. Susan was well wrapped in a blanket over her pyjamas and had eaten reasonably well. Paul had eaten very well when he arrived home from school.

As Linda put out the food for her meal and Bob's she began to tell him about her day. They ate in the kitchen in the evenings during the week; at weekends the whole family had meals in the dining-room to make the most of their togetherness.

Bob failed to find comfort in Linda's greeting or in the bright kitchen with its white peninsular table and attractive mats and the tall wineglasses. Linda scoured the supermarkets for bargains and kept a little notebook with the names of the wines and marks out of ten.

An invitation to a christening had come in that morning's post. Of course she knew Bob would be unlikely to be able to go. She would have to take the children on her own. Being Linda she had already decided that they would travel by train and she had consulted the timetable and checked on the fares. She had also seen a dress in a shop window which looked like the very thing to wear. She was full of enthusiasm and intended to talk Bob round into not minding her tripping off to London with the children, and being godmother to her cousin's baby.

The wine was poured and the pie, crisp and brown, was on the table. Linda decided to lead into the subject of the christening by way of other topics.

'The self-defence classes are going well,' she said as she served the vegetables.

'What self-defence classes?' asked Bob.

'Ours—the ones we got going.'

Suddenly Bob was on the alert. What on earth was his wife talking about?

'Say that again, Lindy-lou?'

She stopped serving, her tablespoon in mid-air, full of carrots.

'I don't believe I've mentioned them, now I come to think. You've been so busy lately.'

'What on earth have you been doing?'

Something in his voice and face was unlike her husband, her Robert. She felt strangely guilty.

'One day Lucy Grindal called, she wanted your advice on what we, the women of the city, could do against this attacker. She thought of self-defence classes. Julia had thought of those too, so I rang her and she came round and we talked about it and got them organised and they are running nicely.'

'Linda, you've always been a model policeman's wife, what on earth possessed you?' His voice was cold as ice.

She looked at him and words came into her mouth only to falter on her tongue and prove unpronounceable.

He shook his head, unable to believe it. 'You must have been mad. Thank goodness the press haven't got hold of this. Policeman can't protect his own wife, she has to form self-defence classes! I can't believe it of you, Linda. You must have been out of your mind. I know the whole female population has been going potty, but for you to stab me in the back like this ...!'

He pushed his plate away.

'Bob—darling—of course—I can see that construction might be—'

'Damn well would be. How could you forget yourself like that? Sabotage my career. Make me a laughing stock.'

She had never seen him so angry, and with her!

'Oh, Bob, I didn't ... I haven't ...'

'We are part of each other, Linda. A team. Can't be separated. You've brought discredit on us.'

'Nobody knows! Well, Lucy and Julia...'

'And any women who have joined your class, and the caretaker of whatever place they are held in, and Old Uncle Tom Cobley and All ...'

'Bob, don't look at me like that!'

He pushed his plate even further away, stood up, and left the table.

'I'm not hungry, Linda.'

He walked out of the kitchen.

Linda looked down at the table and her eyes brimmed with tears. She could see how foolish she had been, how it looked to Bob. The tears refracted the wineglasses so that they seemed to swim and sparkle. She felt a strong impulse to sweep them off the table and throw the pie and vegetables down after them. But she didn't. She controlled herself. Her appetite had gone, too. She was angry, yet felt guilty. If a policeman's lot is not a happy one, that of a policeman's wife is infinitely worse, she thought. Talk about Caesar's wife having to be above reproach. What about the wife of a normally sweet and lovely detective chief inspector? The worst of it was that she knew Bob was absolutely right. Looking back on that delightful late summer afternoon, remembering the feeling of solidarity and of striking a blow for a good cause, the feeling of sisterhood, Linda realised for the first time that the life of a policeman's wife is essentially a solitary one. She does not have the same freedom as other women. The job comes with the man, and if you want one you have to accept the other. Tough.

It took the whole evening for things to calm down between them. Neither was willing to speak a word. Linda took the children up to bed, Bob went upstairs and read to them, he had a bath while he was up there and then came down and sat in his chair in stony silence.

Linda wasn't going to be the first to

speak. The words he had spat at her earlier rang through her head. She hugged them to her bosom as Cleopatra hugged the asp. She switched on the television, something they hardly watched at all. They sat without speaking to each other and without taking in the sense of what they were seeing. It was a famous film from the sixties but it might as well have been Donald Duck. Which of them was going to give way and speak first, that was the question.

The film ended. The news came on. First the national news, then the local news. The murder in York hadn't made the national news but during the local news there on the television Bob's face flashed up, and the whole scene at the media conference earlier that day. At the table with Bob was Bruno Hallam, looking as though he was listening intently.

Bob was speaking earnestly, his eyes looking straight at the camera and into Linda's soul. Then the scene changed to the streets of York, with an interviewer pushing a microphone into people's faces and asking for their opinions. The item ended and Linda switched off the set. Turning impulsively, she said, 'I'm sorry, dear.'

He looked at her and his face was no longer frozen.

'I'm bloody hungry,' he said, and smiled.

'Let's put the pie in the microwave.'

'Let's.'

They moved in unison into the kitchen and put the meal to warm up as though they were well-rehearsed partners in a ballet.

'I had a letter from my cousin Meg this morning,' she said. 'They are calling the baby Laura and she's invited us to the christening, in about a month's time. I guess you won't be able to go but I would like to, if you don't mind looking after yourself for a couple of nights. It would hardly be worth going for less, it's quite a journey.'

'If I know you, Linda, you have already found out times of trains and fares and all the rest of it.'

'Yes,' said Linda. 'And I saw a dress in a shop window, with some matching accessories. I think the outfit will be ideal, and only two hundred.'

'Sure,' said Bob, without the vaguest delight.

'Of course I will have to get some new shoes as well,' she added.

'Good,' said Bob.

Linda wondered whether he was with her or mentally still down at the police station, but she began to serve up the pie for the second time.

'Come on, darling!' she said. 'Thing's aren't that bad!'

'They are, you know.'

'Sorry?'

'Oh, nothing. It's not been a good day.'

'Mine's not been perfect. The clothes-line broke and the clothes got grubby.'

'Linda, I'm working on a murder case and you go on about a broken clothes-line!'

'I thought we'd finished quarrelling,' said Linda.

166

'And you intend to spend three hundred quid!'

'Two hundred,' she corrected.

Linda was shaken. She and Bob were having a row, a real row, and she had taken such trouble with the meal. When the quarrel had seemed to be over it was starting up again. She didn't mind about the clothes-line. She didn't care about the new outfit, she could wear the green *again*. But she did care about Bob.

'Come on, tell me?' she asked, putting her hand on his wrist. She loved his wrists. Perhaps wrists would be the next erogenous zone.

Bob wanted to draw his hand away but he didn't. The pie was delicious and he felt like finishing the little that was left. It was easier than trying to explain. Why was he taking it out on Linda?

'I don't mind you spending the money,' he said.

'I know you don't. You're always telling me to spend more on myself. But something has got to you. It's your boss,' she added, inspired.

'I'll be lucky to have a boss soon. Only yesterday there was talk about redundancies, particularly at my level. It seems they want to cut out the middle men.'

'This is idiotic, darling. They won't make you redundant.'

'They might well.'

'They won't.'

'The squad could manage without me.'

'No, they couldn't. They haven't got your experience.'

'Experience counts for nothing unless you use it.'

'What do you mean?'

'I might as well tell you. This afternoon at our briefing meeting Bruno appeared and asked what I had done about the new list of sex offenders missing from various areas, who might be on our territory. There is one in particular who could cause great concern. "What list?" I said. He went white. "The one Jester circulated today," he said, very quietly. Or words to that effect. I thought I would awaken in a cold sweat, relieved that it was a bad dream, but

168

no, I stood there with not a word to say. Thing is, Jester—you know James Jester, Linda—had circulated the list; I couldn't recall it, and I found out afterwards that there had been an error on his part, he'd accidentally missed me off the circulation label. He thought I'd already seen it.'

'You mean James Jester didn't pass information to you that he should have done, but did pass it to Bruno Hallam?' Linda was ready to enter the lists against Jester, whom she had always liked until now.

'It was an oversight. I gave Jester hell about it. Threatened to send him to uniform branch.'

'Was it an attempt to curry favour, office politics?'

'No, no, I'm sure it was pure accident. He's been exhibits officer, general dogsbody, and also working with this offender-profiling team. Long hours. He thought I'd already seen the paper. Simple enough.'

Linda didn't think it was simple. She still had some pie on her plate but now didn't feel much hunger for it.

'It was unfortunate,' she said, 'but surely there's no need to talk about losing your job.'

'If there are redundancies I'll be on the list.'

'No, Bob. One failure of communication won't make any difference. It isn't like you to be in a mood like this. I've never known you anything but positive.'

'Linda, if I had seen the list there was one man I would be searching heaven and earth for. Having heard his name we all realised that the recent murder in Leeds could have been committed by him. It could also be connected with our series.'

'Don't get emotionally involved, isn't that what you advise—'

'Bruno flew from Leeds on Saturday ... flew from Leeds ... got a lift in one of the bloody helicopters that was coming our way—that's a joke, I could drive to Leeds in forty minutes.'

'Perhaps *he* did that one! While he was there!' said Linda, trying to jolly up the tone. Her husband ignored her.

'At least he *went* there by train, saved

the department a quid or two.'

They finished their meal in silence. As they cleared the table together, Bob, regaining some of his usual attitude to life, felt he ought to show some interest in her proposed new outfit.

'You don't go in for dresses,' he said. 'You're normally in jeans and trainers.' There was the hint of regret in his voice which was often there when he mentioned her clothes.

'It does me good to make myself pretty sometimes,' said Linda. She expected him to respond with a little compliment, and looked at him in surprise when he said nothing, so she went on, 'I thought if I bought it, it would come in for later, Christmas isn't so far away. It is a warm colour, sort of plum, and very simple, the new length everyone has been wearing during the summer. Shaped to the figure and a flowing skirt.'

'Good,' said Bob. 'Flowing skirt sounds attractive. Get it while you have the chance. If I'm out of a job we might have to be more careful.'

Linda left the bottle of wine on the table. If they finished it off later, it wouldn't matter.

When she was sitting knitting by the fire and Bob was opposite with his head back and eyes closed, listening to music, she asked quietly, 'What difference does not seeing the list make? Really?'

He opened his eyes instantly and she knew he had not been able to concentrate on his favourite composer.

'Who can tell? I've told you there is one name on it who according to his *modus operandi* could be our man,' he said. 'We are searching through haystacks for needles at the moment. Very time-consuming. I can't see them keeping so many staff on for long. But when the attacks start again—and they will—there will be a public outcry. Someone is going to be pilloried if we haven't caught the murderer and that person will be me.'

'You think the attacks are going to go on?' Linda's voice was very quiet.

'I'm sure of it. We have had these periods of calm before. Oh, I don't think having killed will stop him.'

'Did anything else happen at the meeting?' Linda asked.

'Well, yes. Hallam said he had really come to tell us about some new equipment he is keen to try out. Thinks it will make us more efficient. Derbyshire are trying it. It is a mobile voice-and-data system, slashes the time spent on crime reporting. Apple MessagePad, they call it. Cellnet and BT worked on the project. You have this little pad with you and send reports from the scene back to base, where they download the info on to computer. Quite tiny to carry, a hand-held computer you could say, with a GSM phone. Saves writing reports, and you know what a drag they are.'

'Sounds terrific,' said Linda. 'Only mind you don't finish up like the White Knight in *Through the Looking-Glass*, all hung round with various bits of equipment.'

'We are waiting to hear how Derbyshire make out with it, and if they are pleased, we'll try it ourselves.'

Linda went on knitting, thinking that first thing in the morning she must make some telephone calls to free herself from all involvement in the self-defence classes. It was a pity, but she saw Bob's point and there was no help for it.

Bob did not have a nightmare that night, but he did have a dream. He dreamed he was in the neighbourhood pub with his pal from next door, Tom Churchyard. It must have been Thursday. Bruno Hallam came in. He came up to Bob and offered to buy a round. In the dream Bob could taste the beer. Then Bruno apologised for humiliating him. It was a good dream.

Then the radio-alarm began to chirrup softly and he woke to reality.

It was the morning when, on her way back from her run, Angela saw two young moorhens fighting—running at one another, rising in the air as they did so—and clashing together, exactly like the old pictures of fighting cocks.

The other students walked past under the covered way without pausing. Only Angela stood fascinated. She stepped out of the shelter of the canopy and watched the two young fowl as they went through clash after clash. At last one, the younger and smaller of the two, ran off defeated.

Before the victor had time to strut about and enjoy his success, a larger, older bird appeared from nowhere, grabbed him by the neck and downed him with a single movement, just as a wrestler throws an opponent. Once released, the poor little victor, so soon after his victory a victim himself, ran off in a frightened and crestfallen manner.

Angela waited a few seconds before going herself, but the tiny drama of aggression seemed to be over. She realised how cold it was and rubbed her hands together, then began to jog in the direction of hot coffee.

8

It was the middle-aged woman called Lucy Grindal who found the severed head.

Lucy's father, Canon Grindal of York Minster, was away at a conference about young offenders. As his daughter and only surviving child, she spent much of her time looking after him—Canon Grindal was not as young as he had been, as they say. In fact he would soon merit the adjective 'aged' though no one would dare to imply that to his face.

For the few days of the conference there was no need for Lucy to be at home, so she had gone to stay with her friend Jane, who had just had flu. Being Lucy, she took two of her dogs with her. Being Jane, the friend didn't mind. The dachshunds were the price of Lucy's company and part of it, like cheese with biscuits or cake with wine.

In the morning early, before Jane was awake, the gentle touch of the dogs' damp cold noses woke Lucy while the sky was still dark and all the houses wrapped in sleep.

'Oh, no, Rupy! Clemmy!' she protested. 'Get off. Go to lie down again on your blanket. It is too early. Shhh! Be quiet!'

But half an hour later she had given up the idea of sleeping. She heaved herself out of bed and into her old dog-walking clothes. She could have a bath later. Looking out, Lucy saw that the sky was now a paler shade of black, 'nearly black', as they describe ladies' stockings, and that a light had appeared in a neighbour's kitchen. Jubilant dogs and reluctant Lucy went out into the cold and made their way towards a road she had discovered not far from her friend's house. It was a link road which was gradually falling prey to commerce.

The thick untrimmed hawthorn hedges, furred with bare prickly twigs and branches, rose at the back of a wide grass verge. In front of the hedge a few small ornamental trees grew, untended and unpruned, in the rough winter grass. Both Prince Rupert and Clementina Crosspatch were on leads, and she was longing to let them off for a free scamper, but now and then headlights split the darkness and the swoosh of a car, or the steady roar of a heavy goods vehicle storming down the long straight road, made the risk of the dogs running into their path too much to take. Instead they plunged here and there on the end of their leads, trying to drag Lucy after enticing smells of rabbit under the hedge, and she stumbled along over the tussocks of dying grass. If only she could have let them run free, the cold, clear air and the faint remaining aroma of autumn, with the paling stars and moon above, would have refreshed her spirit.

She walked down the long road on the overgrown verge and it began to seem endless. Then she reached an area of warehouse-type shops, deserted at that time in the morning. There was a large spread of car-parking in front. It was a relief to walk off the road, past the barrier to keep out cars, bend down and release the catches from the two dogs' collars and stand up free. After a moment she began to walk again, the dogs in orbit round her as their centre.

The gradual light of day and the fact that her eyes had become accustomed to the conditions enabled her to see the blocks of buildings ahead, and the mesh of the railings on her right, round a square flooded depression in the ground which gleamed through encroaching reeds. Between wire mesh and wall an opening seemed to lead to more rough grass and more tall thorn hedge, but this looked quiet, secluded and safe.

Lucy walked ahead saying, 'Here, Rupy, here, Clemmy,' and sure enough, when she had edged between the huge oil tanks and past a few thick cables, she found she was right. At the back of the buildings lay a decent strip of longish grass and a comfortable overgrown hedge, an ideal sniffing-around place for dogs. They quartered the ground busily as she stood and rested for a few minutes. As the last of the moonlight met the first light of the sun, that pre-dawn growing clarity, she could pick out every detail in this narrow forgotten area where she could walk next to the buildings on a gravelled path.

She hadn't quite reckoned with what she would find. She saw the pale rounded shape of the head with its long flaxen hair before the dogs did. A blow seemed to strike her breastbone and it was as if her heart stopped with fear and pity. Clinging to the wall, frightened by her own reaction, she thought it would be an inconvenient place for her to die. In that first shock she was sure the head was that of a baby or a small child. The dogs ran up to it and snuffled at it eagerly, their tails wagging with excitement. As she walked over to them, they lost interest and wandered off on the trail of a rabbit.

At least it wasn't a human head, although it was big enough to belong to a baby or a small child. She gradually realised that it was the head of a doll. She could see it in profile now, and in another stride she could see the full face—and the face was very like that of a little girl about two years old. If it had lain there pristine, it would not have been so disturbing. The long blonde hair was tangled round the head and spread out behind it. The head had been detached from the body. Lucy looked round. There was a fair amount of litter on the grass, but the body of the doll was nowhere to be seen. Her eyes were drawn back to the head. Somehow attached to its rudimentary neck was a crumpled shape of muslin. At first it had looked like doll underclothing but then she realised it was more like a ghost shape of a doll body. Without stuffing to make it firm and round, or top clothes to hide it, this weird transparent remnant, now a wisp of whitish colour on the ground, turned Lucy's stomach over. Together with the soiling of some kind over the upper face and the front hair, it gave the head its aura of death and—above all—of desecration.

A doll. She had always thought there was something scary about dolls and this one had been the object of some pervert's attentions. The soiling on the upper face did not look like mud or anything as innocent. She shivered slightly in the cold morning air as the warmth of walking gradually left her. From thinking of perverts she thought of the so-called Ripper. Had he done this? Would it be a clue for the police? Lucy had become very police-orientated since the death of the Dean in his own cathedral had changed her world. She stood for some time as the dogs amused themselves, running to her now and then, giving the doll's head a sniff in passing, before returning to their quest for rabbits.

I had better go back to Jane's, she thought at last. She will be waking and wondering where I am. Though of course when she sees the dogs aren't in the house she will know what I am doing. Still, I had better be going back.

Unwilling to be influenced by her emotions she sturdily carried on with the walk, going to the end of the buildings and round on to the farthest end of the car-park, where she put the dogs back on their leads. In a couple of minutes she would be on the main road and heading back past bungalows and semi-detached houses towards her friend's home. Instead of doing this, she found herself standing still again, indecisive, unable to move.

It would seem ridiculous, Lucy Grindal thought, to report this find to the police. On the other hand, if the mess on the doll's forehead was what she thought it was, it might be valuable forensic evidence of a psychopathic personality. She would look an awful fool if she reported it. Would that matter, if the doll itself provided useful evidence? Suddenly the decision was made. She might as well report it, after all. If she looked a fool, did it matter? It wouldn't be the first time. But it was no use just telling them, sending them out here on what might be a wild-goose chase, if in the meantime someone had cleared up this area and the evidence was gone. She would have to take the head with her.

Lucy fastened the dogs to a post, turned, and retraced her steps to where the head was lying. In her pocket (among numerous other things) she always kept some clear plastic bags, the kind she acquired round vegetables from the greengrocer. They were flimsy, soft enough to fold into a tiny space and big enough for the purpose. She carried them to use as pooper-scoopers when that was necessary. Now she fished a handful of them out and selected a large one. Then she slipped her hand inside it. The task she had set herself was hardly bearable, but she was convinced it had to be done. If the head *had* been that of a child it could hardly have seemed more distasteful to her. She grasped the hair of the doll through the thin plastic of the bag and lifted the head, then neatly inverted the bag over it, so that the messy mass was now inside. She had a slightly larger translucent bag with handles and slipped it inside that. It wouldn't be the easiest of tasks, completing her walk with one hand holding the leads of two lively dogs and the other holding the bag. It wasn't. It was difficult and tiring. She was relieved to meet nobody close enough for them to see what her burden was. A couple of men passed in the distance going off to work in the dawn, and the passenger in a four-wheel drive car looked at her curiously as he was driven past, but she could ignore that.

Luckily Jane, weak from flu, was still upstairs when Lucy let herself back into the house. She found an opaque carrier bag and put the wrapped head in it, then went to her bedroom and laid it next to her spare shoes. The previous night she had done all her packing, except for her toilet things, which she needed a while longer. Prince Rupert and Clementina Crosspatch were tired and satisfied by their walk; after a drink and a Bonio each, they lay down and went to sleep as if conscious of work well done.

Lucy went and had a bath and then, dressed tidily in a tweed skirt in blue and grey and matching blue cashmere jumper, embellished by a necklace of lapis lazuli and other semi-precious stones set in silver, she put on one of Jane's aprons and began to prepare breakfast. She took a cup of tea upstairs to Jane and soon she could hear footsteps overhead and thought it was time to begin cooking the bacon.

'Did you enjoy your walk?' her friend asked later over the bacon and eggs. Looking round the neatly pretty breakfast table, she added, 'I shall miss you, Lucy, and these delicious breakfasts.'

'I always cook bacon and eggs for Father,' Lucy replied absent-mindedly. She had decided not to mention the doll's head to Jane.

'You spoil him.'

'Well, why not? I have a weakness for cooked breakfasts, too. Yes, thank you, I did enjoy the walk. We went down the link road as a change from the suburban roads.'

'I wouldn't have enjoyed that. Rather boring, don't you think so? It is more fun to look at everyone's front gardens and see how different they are, and what flowers are coming out.'

Lucy didn't answer. She had the excuse that her mouth was full, so nodded in acknowledgement.

'Your visit has done me so much good,' said Jane. 'It is exactly what I needed, to be coddled for a little while and not have to look after myself.'

'You did very well, managing on your own through the worst of the flu,' said Lucy. 'I only wish I could have come earlier.'

'Actually it wasn't too bad. Of course I felt awful but not really like eating, drinking or talking, you know. I tottered into the bathroom to fill the kettle now and then and at the beginning I had taken all sorts of drinks and things up into the bedroom, knowing what the flu would be like. The central heating was on full and I had the radio and that small telly when I felt fit enough to need company. Various tablets as well. I wouldn't have wanted you to catch it.'

'Convalescence can be the most difficult time to be on your own,' agreed Lucy. 'Anyway, you are stocked up now. There is enough food in the fridge and deep-freeze to last a siege. Even if you were snowed up for a fortnight you would be all right. I will ring every day to see how you are and I can always pop over for an hour in the car.'

'You are wonderful,' said Jane gratefully, and Lucy replied with a smile that it was nice to be appreciated.

'But now I must be off,' she said after washing up. 'Father is due back later and I have some business in town to do on the journey home.'

On her way home she was going to call at the police station with the severed head, and ask to see either DI David Smart, or DCI Robert Southwell. She'd got to know both of them when the Dean died.

It was about an hour later when she entered the police station on Clifford Street and made her request at the counter.

She had had difficulty finding somewhere to park, and there was quite a way to walk even when she had parked. Prince Rupert and Clementina Crosspatch were with her because Lucy felt she needed moral support. The plastic bag felt heavy in her hand, and the thought that she was making a fool of herself good and proper kept niggling at her mind. Somehow, though, she had gone on walking until she reached the side entrance and went through the double doors into the busy police station.

'I have called to see either DCI Southwell or DI Smart,' she said firmly, suppressing the trembling she felt. The constable on duty tried to persuade her to see an ordinary uniformed officer, but she held out for one of the two men she knew. She didn't fancy having to explain her hunch to anyone else. Lucy could be commanding when she liked and in the end the PC on duty rang upstairs to the detective inspectors' office and asked for Dave.

'Who is it?' Dave Smart asked in an irritated voice. He had enough on without stray civilians cropping up demanding to speak to him.

'A Miss Lucy Grindal, sir, with two dogs and something in a carrier bag.'

'Dachshunds?' asked Dave.

'Those sausage dogs, sir.'

'I know who she is. They can be fierce, those dogs, I know from experience. Please ask her if she will speak to me on the telephone.'

The constable turned to Lucy. Yes, she would speak on the telephone.

'I found this head, Mr Smart,' she said diffidently, but firmly. 'It's a doll's head, but it has been desecrated in some way I don't like, and I think as you are on the attacker enquiry you ought to check it just in case.'

Dave remembered her perfectly from that time the Dean had died unexpectedly in the Minster. He spoke now in a pleasant and friendly way.

'I'm busy, Miss Grindal, and Mr Southwell is out of the office at present, but would you mind passing the item over to Detective Constable Jester? Have you met him before? I assure you we will check it out carefully. Please give him exact details of where you found it, time, everything.'

Lucy sat down and in a minute a tall, gangling young man appeared. He had unruly red hair, a long boyish face with a few freckles and an earnest, pleasant, but worried expression. James had been so thoroughly ticked off by his beloved boss, DCI Southwell, that he was considering leaving the force. He introduced himself politely to Lucy, and sounded intelligent. Lucy explained and then handed him the bag. He took it in his long fingers—she noticed his wrist bones were showing, shooting out from his shirt-sleeves—and he couldn't stop himself shuddering.

'What's the matter?' asked Lucy.

'It's only that—plastic carrier bags—they give me the willies, that's all.' He smiled apologetically.

'They are very ordinary things,' said Lucy, who didn't know anything about the role a plastic carrier bag had played in his life.

'I will get over it,' said James Jester. 'I am ashamed of being such a baby.' But he peeped inside the bag, saw the vague outline of the head through its shroud of translucent plastic, and shuddered again. Of course it couldn't be what it looked like, or this nice middle-aged lady would have told him, or Mr Smart would have—she had said *doll's* head, hadn't she ... but it looked ... it certainly did look ... gruesome ...

Lucy had been watching him intently.

'It does look like that, doesn't it?' she asked in sympathy. 'Stop it, Rupy and Clemmy, the constable doesn't want to be sniffed at. Sit, good dogs. It's all right, it is a doll, really it is. It has been soiled, disgustingly. I think you ought to check it out. You'll see why when you unwrap it. You will agree with me, I feel sure.'

One and all, the squad on the enquiry did agree with her. They did see why. The sight of the thing made them feel every bit as queasy as James Jester had. The mess on the doll's forehead and front hair was ... semen ... well, it looked like that, plus some other kind of soiling they couldn't identify as readily. Whoever had detached and desecrated the doll's head must be sick and should be found, whether or not he was the 'Ripper'.

'Where did she say it was?' Dave Smart asked. He was irritable because the head made him feel disturbed, shaken. Ridiculous. The things he'd seen, to get upset over a doll's head! 'We'll have to make a thorough search,' he went on, 'in case there's something else.'

Jester referred to his notes. 'Miss Grindal found it at the back of a surplus goods store on the Murtwick link road. She squeezed between the fuel stores and over some cables to get on to this bit of grass. It sounds a very odd thing to do.'

'Funny place for a respectable clergyman's daughter! Raking about at the back of warehouses! Climbing over cables! And what time of the morning was this? Good job none of our patrols saw her!'

'She explained that she went there to let the dogs run about, away from the traffic.'

'Doggy people!' Dave Smart said. 'They do the most extraordinary things. Whatever do they want to keep the animals for in the first place? Get out there with a team, James. Give the area a good going over, this grass behind the building, see what else you can find. It may be all a waste of time but we can't afford to neglect anything. *Now.* You never know, it could prove to be the lead we have been waiting for.'

Lucy's description was exact and within half an hour a team of police had cordoned off the area in question. The long thin strip of grass behind the 'factory shop' was littered with quite a few scraps of paper and other debris, which the police team started carefully gathering up. Much of it was the most ordinary kind of rubbish, sweet wrappers, cigarette packets, expanded polystyrene containers for junk food. The only unusual things they found at the first sweep were several detached pages from a sex magazine, showing the wives of the readers, in suggestive poses. Some of the team stopped work to have a good look at these before being brought to order by their sergeant.

'Well, sarge, would you send up photos of your missus for everyone to gawp at?' one of the constables asked.

'I wouldn't but that's not the point,' was the reply. 'We're here to do a job. Keep them, since it's a sex attacker we're after. With your fingerprints all over them we might start to think you are the criminal, though, sunshine.'

It was at the end of thirty minutes—not bad time as these searches go—that they found something relevant to the doll's head, and then it was in the longer undergrowth beneath the hedge, which had not been covered during the first check. The find was a single doll's leg, or rather part of a leg, the end with the foot. Also a round shaggy white beret, doll-size, together with the light brown cardboard core from a toilet roll, all lying in a little group one on top of the other.

'No use to us, really,' said Dave Smart. 'Attacking a doll isn't criminal behaviour, but not normal either. Take swabs, James, and keep them in the fridge pending a decision. They might well be sent to Wetherby presently, when we catch him. If nothing else it might give evidence of mental state.'

It seemed to Dave and to Jenny Wren that a long time had elapsed since her car was scrawled with paint. The murder enquiry had swamped everything else, but Dave remembered what Southwell had said about the writer being hate-filled, and the possibility—a long possibility, certainly—that he was the man they were after. Dave decided to raise the matter.

'I haven't forgotten him,' said Southwell. 'Things have mounted up. With that last list from our intelligence office you know we have been actively searching for three men, particularly Spendlove. But we can have this stupid poisonous graffiti expert in for questioning. Get him in, Dave. I want the interview phrased so that we find out if he was in the area of the murder at the time. How is Jenny? Anything else occurred?'

'She has gone very quiet about the whole thing. Her car is back in use but she is parking in a different place every day.'

'Very shaken,' concluded Bob.

'She isn't over it yet. Afraid of something else happening.'

'Oh, and one more thing, Dave. I authorise the swabs from the doll's head to be sent for DNA testing.'

9

Things were frantic in Clifford Street the following morning. A new attack had taken place. Southwell had been notified at home in the early hours and as soon as he reached his desk he asked for the details.

'The Dutch House?' he said in surprise. 'Lightning striking twice?'

'The lady is alive and fairly well,' said Sergeant Diamond.

The names of the dwellers in the Dutch House complex ran through Bob's mind. It was very close to his own home. The lovely old seventeenth-century house, a small gem among historic houses, was privately owned by Miss Cherry Ducket-Penrose and was open to the public. The Victorian wing and the stables had been converted into a number of flats and one of these was the home of Linda's friend Julia Brandsby. Before Sergeant Diamond

197

told him the name, Bob had an intuition that Julia was the victim of the attack.

'Mrs Julia Brandsby,' said Terry Diamond.

His boss looked at him attentively and waited.

'She was attacked at the rear of the flats late last night, but managed to crawl back to her house and ring us. Since then of course she has been down at the hospital for checks and been examined also by a police doctor. A counsellor is with her now. We are going out to get her statement directly.'

'She's a close friend of my wife's, you know, Terry.'

'Yes, Mr Smart told me that, sir.'

'Linda will want to go to her to see if she can do anything to help. I'd better ring home.'

Bob did not have the chance to make a private call for some time. When he did ring, the phone shrilled out to an empty house. Bob sat with the instrument to his ear as he made notes with his other hand. At last he put it down. There was no way he could tell her until she arrived home.

He felt surprised that she was out. Surely she hadn't left Susan on her own? Though if she had only slipped to the shops ...

As Bob sat at his desk fuming quietly to himself, his wife Linda and his little daughter Susan were walking from their suburb of Clifton towards the centre of York. It was a bright and sunny morning and Susan was recovering well after her short but nasty bout of flu. Her mother thought a breath of air and a bit of exercise would do the child good, so Susan was wrapped up warmly against the cold and they were both enjoying the walk. They were hoping to meet friends, at least Linda's friends, for there are times, out of the tourist season, when York goes back to the character of a large village. Then you can count on meeting people you know as you walk round the shops and down the ancient streets with their curious old Viking names, like Goodramgate, Coppergate, Gillygate—but hardly anyone spares a thought for St Giles, whose church there gave that street its name, or the coopers of Coppergate, or the spur makers of Spurriergate. Linda and Susan certainly weren't thinking of ancient times at all.

'Where are we going first, Mummy?' asked Susan.

'I thought we would go to the market and find some pretty wool for a new jumper for you,' said her mother.

'What is it going to have on it?' asked Susan, for Linda's knitting was rapidly reaching cult status in the Southwell household and the nearby school. Paul had a black jumper with golden stripes which made up the body of a tiger without needing any outline for the beast. Susan mostly had Scandinavian designs that winter because she loved the little multi-coloured patterns and helped choose the colours and decide which went with which.

'What about ...' Linda pretended to shut her eyes as she stood still on the pavement for a second. 'Let's think ... I know, darling, what about a row of hearts round the bottom edge and another across the yoke at the top and round the wrists above the ribbing.'

'Yes, please, Mummy!'

Susan was a satisfactory little girl to have. She was always ready to like her mother's ideas and although her fights with her brother gave promise of an extreme form of Women's Lib to come in adulthood, she was docile on the whole, pretty, and liked being close to people she loved. She had been a cuddly baby and was a cuddly child, not like her brother Paul who had wriggled off the knees of fond adults at the age of seven months and never been interested in wriggling back on again.

'You see,' Linda explained to her daughter, 'this is the day they will be selling knitting wool in the market, so let's go there first and buy the wool.'

'Don't they sell wool in shops?' asked Susan.

'They do, but it is cheaper in the market.'

By the time they reached the market, tucked away behind Parliament Street which it had once filled with its shouting and clutter and excitement, Linda noticed

201

that the weather was changing, and she doubted her wisdom in bringing Susan out. From being a pleasant sunny morning it was developing into a cold windy day. The market was fairly protected but the canvas awnings were flapping and creating worrying cracking sounds in the gusts. The shoppers looked up in alarm when this happened over their heads, and some of them were rushing their purchases and then making for home.

Linda and Susan found the best stall for knitting wool and Linda bought a vast skein of pretty mohair in shades of mauve and mist, weighing half a kilo, which she intended for a garment for herself. There didn't seem to be what she wanted for Susan.

'I'll tell you what, dear,' she said, 'a new knitting-wool shop has opened on Castlegate. You were asking about shops. There isn't as much choice as usual here, let's go and see what we can find indoors before we head for home.'

She was feeling worried about Susan becoming worse instead of better for her outing. They had already seen several women they knew and stopped for brief chats, and it was during these stationary intervals that she had noticed the child shivering. Then Linda caught sight of another friend in the crowd.

'Julie!' she called out, for Julia Brandsby did not seem to have noticed her. 'Julie!'

There was still no response. Julia was moving rapidly away and appeared to be ignoring her, but Linda doubted if her friend would act like that. More, she was sure she wouldn't. There was something strange about this and about the way neat, tidy, self-controlled Julia was walking, clumsily, and stumbling over the edge of a pavement. Pushing between the people and dragging Susan by the hand, Linda chased after her friend. When she was close enough to catch Julia by the sleeve, she was appalled by the face which the other woman turned to her.

'Julie! What on earth is the matter?'

Julia looked dazed and ill. Her face was drawn. She appeared years older. Her coat was not properly buttoned and her scarf was 'all skew-wiff' as Susan would have said. Looking critically up at the adult woman, Susan did think this. She admired Julia as pretty, but not today.

'Oh, Linda ...'

'What is the matter?' Linda said again, very clearly and distinctly. She thought of drugs. No, she couldn't believe it. 'Julia, what is the matter?'

There seemed to be some response at last.

'It's just that ... Oh, Lindy-lou, I've been attacked ...'

'What? Attacked? When did this happen?'

Susan felt the grip of her mother's hand tighten until it was painful.

'Last night ...'

'Last night? What are you doing walking round town?'

Mummy's voice sounds angry, Susan thought. Why was she angry with Auntie Julie?

'I needed to go somewhere ... I couldn't stay at home ...'

Julia and Linda looked at one another in silence.

'Have you told the police?' Linda almost whispered then, matching Julia's faint murmur.

'Yes, of course.'

'Mummy, what's wrong with Auntie Julie?' piped up Susan, penetrating their absorption with her clear high voice.

'I wouldn't want the child to hear ...' said Julia more distinctly.

Linda had been trying to keep all talk of the attacker from Susan's ears during the past months. She glanced down at the child, who looked pinched by the sudden cold wind. The blue eyes were puzzled, enquiring, persistent. What could she do with her for a short time? Of course. They were not far from the Clifford Street police station. This was an emergency, and the police were involved. She could leave Susan with her father for a bit.

'Look, Julie,' she said, taking command, 'we'll have a cup of tea in a quiet spot and you can tell me what happened then I'll put you into a taxi home. There's a café just along here. Come on, you must sit down.'

Julia was in no condition to object. In silence she walked hesitatingly along with them, partly supported by Linda's arm. Once in the café Linda pushed her friend into a chair by a secluded corner table and ordered tea for two.

'Don't you dare stir until I'm back,' she said firmly to Julia and, dragging Susan, darted off towards the police station. When the pair of them arrived at Clifford Street Linda pushed Susan through the station door ahead of herself, followed and looked around her. She knew none of the staff on duty, so had to say who she was and ask to see DCI Southwell.

'Darling,' she burst out as soon as he came into the reception area, looking surprised, 'something's happened.'

'What?' asked Bob, unable to think of anything else to say in the face of her obviously upset state. He had rarely seen his wife like this. The speed of thought, running over their life together, produced in a second the memory of only two crises, both devastating family traumas, which had had the same effect.

'Can Susan possibly stay with you for a few minutes? She's feeling the cold too much, it has started blowing a gale outside. I'll pick her up in ten minutes, I promise.'

'Whatever is the matter?' asked Bob, knowing that there was more to it than Susan feeling cold.

Linda ran her tongue over her lips. How was she to put into words which would get through to Bob all the intricacy of this situation?

'Sit down, Susan,' she said, pushing the child towards a long seat by the wall. 'I want to talk to Daddy for a minute.'

Moving close to Bob, she muttered, 'It's Julia Brandsby. I've just met her and must give her a hot drink and send her home. She's in a dreadful state. She's been attacked.'

'I know. It was late last night,' muttered Bob in reply. He had been reading the report on the incident.

'It must be delayed shock,' said Linda. 'I don't want Susan to ...'

Both parents looked at Susan, who had

begun to play with the buttons on her coat.

'Can you keep her here for a bit?'

'I suppose,' said Bob grudgingly. This sort of thing was not meant to happen. But a look at his daughter's face had decided him. She did look too poorly to be out in the sudden coldness and the wind which had sprung up in the last half-hour. Neither did he want her to hear a distraught Julia telling Linda all the details. Busy at his desk, he had hardly noticed the change in the weather, but it didn't surprise him. The morning weather forecast had predicted a cold front moving from west to east across the country.

'How did you come down?' he asked.

'We walked.' Linda sounded apologetic. 'I thought the fresh air would do her good. It was lovely when we set out.'

'You'd better go home by taxi as well. Don't be long. I'm sure it is against regulations to have children in the nick. Unless they are criminals, of course,' and Bob smiled at his little blonde daughter. Apart from her woeful pale face, she looked pretty. Her winter jacket had a Scandinavian air to it and she was wearing brightly patterned leggings, a woolly hat and mitts. Linda had knitted the hat and mitts. With a feeling of tremendous relief, Linda dashed off back to the café where she had left Julia.

Bob took Susan up to his office, through the general office where most of his staff had their desks.

'You'll have to be good, while Daddy works,' he told her.

Susan took her coat off. Underneath she wore a colourful jumper.

'It's nice and warm in here, Daddy,' she said.

He sat down and pulled towards him the papers he had been working on.

'I know what you can do, sweetheart,' he said. 'My paperclips get in an awful mess. Would you like to tidy them for me? You can do it over there.'

Susan did not want to do it over there. It was not often that she got her daddy all to herself. She wanted to make the most of it.

'Can't I be next to you, Daddy? Let me. Put your paperclips here on the corner of your desk. I'll stand here.'

What she really wanted was sit on her daddy's knee and have a cuddle. But he actually did have urgent work to do. Susan stood at his side and as close to him as she could. She tipped the paperclips from their metal box on to part of the surface of the desk which he cleared for her and began to untangle them. He put his left arm round her and went on with his work, making notes with his right hand. They all had plenty of other work apart from the 'Ripper' enquiry. Before long she was almost on his knee. Her face gradually lost its pinched, white look and became rosy. She was chattering to him and her hair was tickling his cheek. It hung forward on either side of her face in spite of the two small pink plastic slides placed one at each temple.

This is how Bruno Hallam saw them as he unexpectedly walked in at the door. He saw Susan from the back, a view of a colourful child, fair hair forming a curtain. He saw Bob's arm round the little girl, Bob's head touching hers as he bent forward, intent on his work. Bruno heard Susan's voice prattling on, asking how paperclips got themselves in such a tangle, and Bob's preoccupied murmur in reply. It was a tender and loving scene.

Hallam spoke, his voice grating, almost unrecognisable. Bob whipped round, startled, and looked at his superior officer in amazement.

'Get that child out of here,' said Hallam.

His face was chalk-white, his pupils pinpricks in the dark eyes, his thin lips rigid. The words had to force their way out through them. Every inch of his body seemed to be tense with a fury scarcely contained.

The two men looked at one another over Susan's head.

'Of course, sir,' said Bob.

'At once,' said Hallam, biting his words. 'Then see me.'

He turned and left the room and could be heard going upstairs to his own office, leaving behind a bull-like impression of power and anger.

Bob felt a fury of resentment, but he slid Susan from her position half on his knee, his hands with the suspicion of a tremor. Then he got up. Collecting her hat, jacket and mitts, he took his daughter down to the ground floor where uniformed constables were still busy dealing with the constantly varying conditions of traffic in the city. They were using radio, maps and surveillance cameras to do so, in constant touch with their comrades on the beat.

'I hadn't finished your paperclips, Daddy,' Susan had protested as they walked down the stairs.

'I'm afraid the superintendent doesn't want you in the police station,' he replied. 'He is quite right.'

Susan thought her daddy was perfect and it was not possible for anyone else to be as right as he was, but she had noticed the atmosphere Bruno Hallam had created, and she became very quiet. Once back in the entrance area she looked round her with interest.

'Mummy will be here in a minute,' Bob said hopefully. She had said ten minutes. It was twenty already.

In ten minutes more, Linda appeared.

'Something the matter?' she asked at once. The aspect of her husband and daughter told her there was trouble.

'Only that the super doesn't want staff to have their children in the office.'

'Oh-oh!' said Linda. By the look of Bob's face, there had been a very unfortunate incident. She would make him tell her all about it, later. 'Put your jacket on, Susan,' she went on, bending down to help. 'You can do up the buttons perfectly well, a big girl like you. No, they aren't awkward. Just because you aren't well there's no need to be a baby. Come closer, I'll put your hat on for you.'

Long before she had finished these remarks, Bob was gone.

'Then see me,' Hallam had said. Well, he needn't think Bob was going to rush to the superintendent's office like a naughty schoolboy to the headmaster. All right, Susan shouldn't have been there, but it *was* an emergency and Bob could have explained if he had been given a chance to speak. He went first to his own office, fuming. He swept the paperclips off the grey metal edge of the desk into the palm of his hand and tipped them back into their box. He needed a few minutes to calm himself down.

He thought about what he wanted to say to Hallam. The fact that Susan's visit was exceptional and was, surely, harmless. The fact that he himself had not interrupted his work. The fact that it was an emergency.

When Bob finally entered Hallam's office, the super was standing looking out of the window, his back to the door. His hands with their broad palms and sturdy, strong fingers were clasped behind him. When the man turned, Bob could see that he had himself under control, but his face was still white and set, his eyes still angry in a strange way, almost beyond anger, almost into pain. His thin wide lips were still clenched together.

Bob felt within his own body a rising anger. Damn it to hell, he had been the detective superintendent himself for over half a year. Who was Bruno Hallam—himself so recently a chief inspector like Bob—to take such a high-handed tone with him? But another voice within him said calmly, The force relies on discipline within its ranks—otherwise it falls. This internal conflict had been raging for weeks now. The clear calm voice of the old, rational, intelligent DCI Southwell and the new, hot, emotional voice of beleaguered Bob. As usual the calm voice won. He knew that he must conform to the rules. He stood, apparently composed, and awaited events.

'That must not occur again,' Bruno said in a strangely choked voice. 'The working areas of a police station are not the place for any child, let alone the daughter of a DCI. What sort of example are you setting? And you so recently acting detective superintendent and applying for the post?'

Bob thought it had not been necessary to mention this.

'Sir,' he said, stiffly. His nails were

digging into the palms of his hands.

Hallam came towards his own desk and stood behind it, drumming on the surface with his fingers.

'I don't want to discuss this any further,' he said. 'You know my opinion.'

'Yes, super,' said Bob, struggling to keep the sarcastic, insubordinate tone out of his voice.

'All right.'

Bob felt himself dismissed. He waited a second to make sure. Hallam seemed to be looking at the wall.

'Sir,' said Bob. He turned, and left the room.

10

Earlier that day, as soon as Linda had left Susan at the police station, she hurried back to the café where she had left her friend. Julia was still there. The tea had arrived and she had poured herself a cup and had the common sense to sugar it well. She was sitting as if in a trance and cradling the cup in her hands. It had long since gone stone cold.

Linda sat down opposite to her and reached for the teapot.

'It will be stewed,' said Julia. Her voice sounded like the impersonal metallic tones of a computer.

Linda caught the eye of the waitress and said to her, 'A fresh pot of tea, please, fresh cups, and two pieces of that flapjack.'

'You shouldn't be spending money and time,' murmured Julia in a subdued key.

'What are friends for?' asked Linda.

They were silent for a minute, then the fresh pot arrived. The waitress took away Julia's cup of cold untasted tea. Linda waited briefly, lifted the lid and stirred the two tea-bags round in a solemn dance through the hot water, and then poured out two steaming cups from the fresh pot. She sugared one for Julia and put it into her friend's hands, saying firmly, 'Sip it. Come on. Sip it.'

She wondered if it would be wise to sugar her own cup against shock, but disliked sugared tea so much that she didn't; she sipped as she had bade Julia do and then bit into her piece of flapjack. Pushing the small plate bearing the other piece in front of her friend, with a gesture she suggested that Julia eat it. Julia took a half-hearted nibble.

'Last night, I gather?' asked Linda abruptly.

With a sigh, Julia started to speak, slowly and as if the story was being dragged out of her, yet with an inner compulsion driving the narrative forward.

'We've been having a lot of lads climbing

over the wall into the back garden of the flats,' said Julia. 'Well, I say garden. As you know it is only grass and fruit trees, except for the flower bed near the wall. Local lads. Mischief, you know, not real badness. It is not the first time that has happened, by a long way. Several times during my residence at the Dutch House. These are probably the younger brothers of the last lot. They are a nuisance and in the present climate of fear some of the older residents have been really upset by it—the shouting in the night, and the noise of them doing silly things like turning over dustbins.'

'Yes.' Linda's brief word pushed Julia on.

'So. Last night I thought I heard sounds from outside. Naturally enough I assumed that it was the youngsters again and I thought I would go and shout at them. They are easily frightened, you know, if someone stands up to them and sounds really authoritative. Usually, anyhow. I went out. Then there was this blow on the head. It was just above my ear. It is hard to describe how it felt. Sharp pain yet there was something dull about it as if the instrument was thick. It was such a heavy blow that my consciousness faded, contracted into me. I staggered and at once I thought of the attacker. I slipped to the ground. I couldn't help it. He hit me again. It was a man, not the teenage lads.'

'Let me be sure of this. It wasn't in the front near the drive and the herb beds—you were in the back garden of the flats, the part that used to be an orchard, where there are a few apple and pear trees left in the big lawn?'

'I've said that.'

'You must forgive me. I am having trouble taking this in,' Linda said, apologising. Julia hadn't said it, in fact. She had said that was where the lads had been creating a nuisance previously. Linda had learned a lot from her husband.

'That's where I was. Between a couple of the trees. About twelve yards from my own patio.'

'Were you knocked out, do you mean?'

'Not really knocked out. I wasn't

what they call "out cold". Stunned and frightened, but more angry than anything, and surprised. It was almost dark. My sight faded and I couldn't see anything at all. I certainly couldn't do anything to stop him doing whatever he liked, and that is the most frightening thing. Did I tell you he hit me three times?'

'No, you didn't. You've only mentioned twice.'

'I think it was three times,' said Julia as though she didn't really know.

'Julie, before you go on, drink that tea. And eat a bit more of the flapjack. No more talking until you've done that.'

Linda wondered if she had any tablets in her handbag that might be of use. She thought she had aspirin and laxatives and something for indigestion but none of those things seemed very appropriate. Oh yes, and some sore throat tablets.

'Have you got a headache?' she asked, hoping that at least the aspirin might earn its place in her crowded handbag.

'No, not a headache. I don't feel right, but it is not a headache.'

'Would you like an aspirin?'

'I don't think so, thank you, Linda.'

Julia finished her tea and Linda poured her another cup.

'Flapjack,' she said as though she were talking to her children, and pointed to the flapjack still on Julia's plate.

Julia obediently ate her flapjack.

'You were right, Linda. I needed something to eat. Although you mustn't think I've been starving myself. I had some coffee and toast for breakfast.'

When she thought her friend was looking a bit better, Linda said, 'Didn't self-defence classes help at all?'

'I only went to two.'

'Oh, no! What use was organising it if people don't go?' asked Linda.

'I didn't see you there.'

Looking ashamed, Linda admitted, 'No, I didn't go to any. And in fact Bob objects to me having been involved at all. He was furious when he found out. I had to ring up and resign from everything to do with it.'

'So you have a cheek, Lindy-lou,

scolding me for non-attendance.'

'Do you want to tell me any more?'

'I was lying there after he had hit me a few times.'

Linda opened her mouth, but Julia forestalled her.

'I know what you are going to ask. How many times? Well, I don't know how many times he hit me, you have made me realise that.'

'Okay,' said Linda.

'He began to pull at my clothes. He was muttering all the time to himself, in a really nasty voice.'

'Accent?' asked Linda.

Julia thought for a while. 'The police asked me that,' she said, 'and I told them I hadn't noticed any accent. Now that must mean a York accent, mustn't it, if you think about it?'

Linda felt reassured by this speech. Julia was showing signs of improvement, even without the aspirin.

'So you think it was a York accent.'

'But not a strong one. He was talking perfectly good English without much in the way of colloquialisms, so it might have been anywhere in the North of England.' She thought for a while. 'A slight York accent,' she added at last, and nodded.

'And saying?'

'Things like, "They're all the same underneath," and horrible things about women in general. It wasn't in any way personal to me. I was just a female on her own where he happened to be. I can't imagine why he was at the back of our flats. He was pulling at my clothes. My head was full of clouds of pain and the hard earth hurt it. Every bit of me was hurting before it was over. The grass was fairly dry but there was ground frost, there were prints of grass blades on my face and my body, it was cold, oh, so bitterly cold out there, lying on the grass with my jumper pulled up above my breasts and my bra torn off.'

'Torn off? They are tough things to tear.'

'I think he might have used a knife to cut at it. As a matter of fact I have a few cuts in that area. He pulled everything up to my armpits. Then he began to pull down my trousers. He got them down over my hips. In fact right off, in stages. The cold air struck me, harsh like flat knife blades, like dry ice. I was conscious of what was happening most of the time but couldn't do anything about it, still dazed, as if I was in a nightmare and couldn't wake up. I was petrified of what would happen if I did start to fight back, somehow I felt he would become more vicious and violent.'

'You hear sometimes about people who seem to be under anaesthetic during operations, but are conscious and in awful pain and can't communicate,' said Linda.

'I suppose it was like that. Even when I was recovering a bit it seemed best to pretend I wasn't.'

'You were right.'

'I don't know what was for the best, really.'

Julia stopped talking and looked round the café, as though she had never seen it before. The windows were steamed up, the lights were on. The sunny morning had

225

passed like a dream and the day was now dark. Soon it would be winter properly. Vaguely outside she could see huddled figures fighting the wind. Inside there were few customers. Their own voices were so quiet that no one else could hear their conversation above the background music, a pretty bit of Tchaikovsky. The waitress was standing at the till and looked as though she was balancing the takings.

'Go on,' said Linda.

'He tore off my panties and I thought, Here we go, but he made disgusted noises and said horrid things about women, and didn't do anything else, as if he had done all he wanted. Then he said, "It is a pity not many people will be around here," which seemed odd, but I suppose the idea was, he wanted a lot of people to see me stripped, only I didn't feel flattered.'

'Insulted,' said Linda.

'The thing is, at that point I did begin to shout and wave my arms, trying to hit him, trying to get up.' Julia broke down and put her head on the fairly clean table and wept.

'Oh, love,' said Linda, jumping up and going round the table to put her arm round Julia.

After a few seconds Julia sat up again and said in a trembly voice, 'I'm all right.' She mopped at her eyes with her handkerchief.

'And what happened?'

'Well, it was like shouting at the youngsters would have been. I think his crisis, or climax, or trauma, or whatever horrid thing it was, was over, that was it, he'd satisfied something in himself and released his aggression. When he realised I was coming to and fighting he ran off. After a minute or two I crawled back to my flat. On hands and knees, leaving my clothing behind on the grass, what he'd left of it with slashing to get it off. I'd rushed out and left the patio door open. Anyone could have burgled the place, but I was pleased it was open because I could crawl in. I don't know why I crawled because I was quite fit enough to walk. No, perhaps I wasn't. I had to keep stopping, resting, then drag myself a bit further. No, I couldn't have walked.

Then I rang the police. Sitting on the floor all dirty with earth and grass, bruised and battered you might say. They came at once and were very kind. They had to fetch my dressing-gown from the bedroom because I'd passed out on the sitting-room carpet. You have no idea how calm I was then, Linda. A nice policewoman stayed with me for a while and looked after me. They called a doctor and he gave me something to help me sleep. I was so calm it was incredible.'

'Shouldn't they have taken you to hospital, or taken swabs or something?'

'They did all they needed to do, all they thought would be helpful. I did go to the hospital for tests.' Julia screwed her face up, trying to remember. 'Don't worry. The police did all the proper things as far as investigating the attack went. It is only that I can't remember, or can't remember properly.'

'You should have rung me, I would have come at once.'

'I could only think of my own bed and sleep.'

'How did you feel when you woke up this morning?'

'I was worried because I have a lot of work on at present, deadlines for some of it which isn't usual for me. I woke up worried, and tried to make a start as soon as I could. Then it began to scare me, being on my own in the flat. Of course there are the neighbours but I didn't want to have to explain to them. It is so degrading. I thought what I needed was people I didn't know round me, crowds that he would not attack me in. And I thought, Suppose he comes back again—so I came out—and I have such a lot of work on you wouldn't believe, I really can't spare time to come into town. When I actually was among people it all seemed to well up inside and I began to feel really terrible. That's when you saw me.'

'Delayed shock,' said Linda as if she was a medical expert.

'I'm sure you are right.'

'How did you get down? Surely you didn't ride your moped?'

'No, I don't think I could have balanced,

and the car seemed too much trouble, the garage door and everything. I set off, meaning to go to our shops at Clifton probably, then kept on walking until I reached town.'

Linda looked sad, puzzled, impatient. She said, 'I'm going to put you into a taxi. When you get home collect your night things and sponge bag. As soon as I've seen you off I'm going to fetch Susan, then hire a taxi myself for us to go to our house. We will collect you on the way. You are coming to us for the rest of the day and you will have a meal with us this evening and tonight you will sleep in our spare room. You can snuggle down there for the afternoon as well if you feel like it. In fact that might be best. Have you any more of the sedative the doctor gave you?'

'Why should I burden you?'

'Because I insist,' said Linda tersely. 'You will feel a hundred per cent better by tomorrow morning and able to go home again, but give me twenty-four hours to get you over this.'

Well that was a waste of time. I should never have tried behind those flats. Nothing in the newspaper, nothing at all. She was all right, not too skinny like that one that died near the railway line. Perhaps if I'd hit her harder it would have been better, the dead one got lots of publicity. There is more in the paper if they are young. She was a bit old. But that was the point, wasn't it, that they are just as bad if they are old. Those old fat women I got they showed how horrible they are underneath. The old skinny ones are pretty ugly too. But the fat ones are like that little statue they dug up somewhere with rows of curls instead of a face. Faces! They don't need faces. Just those great dugs and fat bellies.

Bob hated what had happened to Julia. It was bad enough when the offences were impersonal for him, strange women. Julia though was a friend, part of the Southwell family life. Her son Adam, now away at university, was a friend too. She refused to tell Adam, Linda said, or let anyone else tell him.

'I want to stay a mother,' Julia had told her. 'A mother-figure. I don't want him to think of me as a sexual being or as a subject for attack. It would harm our relationship.'

She also refused to get in touch with Richard, the retired policeman she had been dating ever since the Southwells' famous dinner party.

Over the next days Bob felt Bruno Hallam's displeasure increasingly. The incident of Susan's presence in the office had never been mentioned again between them, but things happened, or rather didn't happen. A couple of meetings took place without Bob, when he would have expected to be there. He heard members of staff discussing things which he, himself, had not heard of.

So far there was no suggestion of taking him off the 'Ripper' case, but he had the uneasy feeling that such a move could not be far off, even at the very moment when he was on fire to catch the bastard. Well, it was only what he had expected would happen, when Hallam was first appointed.

There was plenty for Bob to do and he knew that being busy was the best plan. He opened the door and said to the nearest officer, 'Find Mr Smart for me, will you?'

'Boss,' said Dave Smart a couple of minutes later, walking in through Bob's office door.

'How is your side of things going at present?' asked Bob. 'The interviews?'

'You know, sir, how busy they're keeping us. Hundreds of them. Quite a lot of the men we've seen more than once. They include people the public have shopped to us, that bloke about Jenny's car, a university man whose wife is accusing him of a violent attack. Miscellaneous. Mixed. All to do with violence towards women.'

'Detail, Dave,' said Bob, sitting down and preparing to listen. 'What I want to know about are those you feel are significant. You and the rest of the team. The more likely ones should be emerging from the ruck by now.'

'A woman came in, assistant in a newsagent's. They have a new lodger in the rooms over the shop. I gather the owner lets the rooms on a rather casual basis, sometimes the place is empty, sometimes every room is full. This youngish man is the only one there at present. He has been there a week and she thinks he is weird.'

'That wasn't much of a basis for getting him in for questioning.'

'No, maybe not. We're not taking any chances. Wouldn't do him any harm to answer a few straightforward questions.'

'What did you decide after seeing him?'

'He *is* weird.'

'That's no answer, Dave.'

'No alibi. Doesn't seem sure what day of the week it is, can't remember where he was any day. We are applying for a search warrant.'

'Next?'

'The bloke who did Jenny's car. Big, burly, loud-mouthed. Swore he didn't do it. Didn't remember Jenny's name or rank. Admits to the near-accident with the schoolchildren. Says he thinks someone did tick him off at the time, but says with the shock he got, nearly running into them, he hasn't any very clear memory of what was said and certainly didn't know the lady who told him off was in the force. We showed him a photograph of what was written on the car. He said he never used language like that, wouldn't dream of it. Again, we're applying for a warrant.'

'Next?'

'The university man. Not sure if he's a lecturer or a professor, can't say I ever found out the difference, never like to ask.'

'And how did he get in on the act?'

'His wife says he's been battering her.'

Dave pushed various papers over the desk. Bob leafed through them, briefly.

'Not Dr Blow?' he exclaimed, pausing for another glance at one sheet.

'Yes.'

'I met him, the time I went up to the university to consult on security, and the warnings they ought to give the women students. Dr Blow is a charming man. I told you about him when we were in the pub once. Could charm the birds off the trees and was certainly doing all right with two very different women. Different types. The tea-lady and one of the provosts.'

'I thought provosts were men,' said Dave.

'They probably used to be.'

'Charming men have been known to knock their wives about.'

'True. Odd, though. What do we know about him?'

'I haven't checked his background, boss. Not yet.'

'Check it, Dave. Any previous accusations from his wife. Ask who saw her and get a copy of the notes on the interview. Usually these blokes are open about their previous careers, we should be able to get hold of the info fairly easily. It will have been published on internal stuff in the uni. Anything else?'

'There is that man, one of the discharged sexual offenders. New to our area. It looks as though his *modus operandi* was similar. Only he went on to rape. Spendlove. His crimes were in the south of England.'

'Been castrated in prison?' Bob's eyebrow went up at a quizzical angle.

'Don't suppose so, boss,' and Dave smiled.

'So what conclusion did you come to on him?'

'It's difficult to tell exactly when he moved north. He's been living like a vagrant, travelling on from place to place. Says he's been contacting friends. He's an old lag. Knows all the tricks. You can tell when you're talking to him, whatever he says is likely to be far from the truth.'

'I know the type.'

At the university Angela Morton was still worrying herself over the relationships between men and women. The next time she wanted to go to the loo after jogging she chose the same cubicle, curious to see again the graffiti which had against her will remained in her head, the piece about the cucumber. Not only was it still there, but other wits had been adding to it.

A cucumber is better than a man because ...

Cucumbers don't put cold feet on you in bed

Cucumbers don't sleep with your sister to see what it is like

Cucumbers don't go to Australia to see their ex-girlfriend and tell you they are just going for a holiday

Cucumbers don't ask, 'Am I the first?'

Cucumbers have more imagination

Cucumbers don't nick the duvet

11

The four men Dave Smart had picked out for further investigation lived within a square mile, but their backgrounds could not have been more different.

The newsagent's shop was in a thirties council estate, nice enough brick-built houses gradually becoming owner-occupied. The shops were in two little parades, facing each other on either side of the bus route, and changed hands fairly often. They had an indefinable air of run-down sleaziness in spite of the efforts of their owners and staffs.

The university was by contrast light, bright, breezy and full of carefully designed detail, bare branches blowing and water rippling. The staff looked well-heeled, confident, the students hopeful and young.

The elaborately built home for tramps had cost half a million. It was staffed by earnest young people doing their best to care for society's vagrant fringe population. Now that it was early winter and the season of giving was approaching, they were appealing for blankets.

The telephone number scrawled on Jenny's car had led the police to a small house in a suburb with snob value. The house was cottagey in character and in other areas might have been demolished to make way for a car-park, instead of rising in value yearly. It had small 'Georgian' panes in the windows and honeysuckle round the door.

The search warrant for this particular house had been put into execution. A notebook had been found, containing miscellaneous bits of information including an account of the near-accident with the schoolchildren. DC Jenny Wren's name was recorded there. Subsequently there were notes of various sightings of her, showing a gradually growing knowledge of her timetable and habits. Each time, the notes used the same filthy adjectives about her. The words scrawled in red paint on her windscreen.

The attacker was making his plans.
This time it is going to be a three-phase campaign. First, start with an ordinary attack or two. They should get more publicity with the new venue. Then—and this is the crux of it—communicate with the police. That makes me excited—yes—just to think of it. Direct contact. Letters, phone calls. Taunting them. I will tell them what I'm going to do and challenge them to stop me. They can't, of course, but they don't realise that yet. Nothing and nobody can stop me, because I am god, all powerful. Then for phase three ...

As the term went on the male population of the university still admired Angela, but didn't seem to get far with her. Many of them were attached to other women so the admiration never went further than an appreciative glance. Among the unattached some were sufficiently stirred to try to get to know her better.

They didn't make any headway.

Angela was always polite and pleasant,

even friendly in a superficial way. A few men took her out. For an hour or two they had the thrill of being her companion as they escorted her to events on the campus or in the town. Then a second invitation found that she was doing something else, unfortunately. The shy smile took the sting out of the refusal. No one was rejected hurtfully, they only failed to become closer.

She went around mainly in groups and made both friends and acquaintances, but no lovers. She sat chatting in bars and coffee shops, enjoyed the sports activities, and formally joined the Women's Group. This damned her at once in the eyes of the male chauvinists.

Tudor Evans, second-year architecture student, didn't think he had a chance. He stood back and observed the progress of events, noticing the fate of other would-be suitors. Like Bruno Hallam, he was a chess player. So Tudor—an inch shorter than Angela Morton, stocky, dark-haired and brown-eyed, bearded, with a skin neither fair nor dark but which tanned easily—set about the business of getting to know her, using tactics and strategy.

She hardly noticed him for a long time. He was only one member of the groups which formed and re-formed and of which she too was a part. Because his course did not overlap with hers at any point, she never saw him at the lectures and seminars she attended. Because his games were tennis, squash and rowing, and her sports were hurdling and running (although she sometimes played mediocre tennis in the summer), they didn't overlap there either. This was winter. The tennis courts were deserted.

He began by observing her movements, discreetly. Before long she had fallen into the habit of lunching at Langwith, often with Jess. There was a certain coffee machine she frequently used mid-afternoon. By being present as part of the landscape, without appearing to notice her, he hoped to become a familiar object and so in a measure accepted. In this he succeeded. Day after day he lunched at Langwith with various friends and gradually a loose kind of circle built up there. Tudor was well liked in his year. If you dropped by the Langwith restaurant in the lunch hour old Tudor would be there, nine times out of ten. It was inevitable as the weeks went by that little incidents would arise; Tudor almost bumped into Angela as she turned away from the serving area with a full cup of coffee; another day his chair was in her way and he moved slightly so that she could squeeze past. The slight apology, the small smile, the air of casual courtesy were all steps on the route.

One day Tudor made a giant leap forward in his courtship, for that was how he thought of it. Angela had not noticed its existence. All the same, his presence had become accepted by her, like the presence of Jess and Mercy, the mandarin ducks and the Canada geese. Of them all, she cared most for the ducks and geese.

When she sat alone for once in the Langwith restaurant, looking at her lecture notes, Tudor collected a cup of tea from the servery and stood beside her table.

'May I join you?' he asked. None of his

usual circle were present at that time.

'Please do,' Angela replied with a brief glance.

'I'm waiting for Charles, do you know him?' Tudor asked as he sat down.

'Vaguely,' said Angela. Charles sometimes went out with Mercy.

'It is our day for site visits,' went on Tudor casually.

Angela really wanted to read her notes, but she had been brought up with good manners, and so she looked at Tudor and gave a slight smile.

'Site visits?' she asked.

Tudor was careful not to let admiration of her show, in either eyes or voice, as he tried to put into layman's language his passion for the buildings of England (and of course Wales).

'We visit small towns and villages and try to trace their organic growth from our own observations without reference to the authorities on the subject. Then afterwards we read up on them before writing a summary, or report. It is a lot of fun.'

Angela looked at him in astonishment.

'Organic growth?' she said. 'But towns and villages are bricks and mortar. They can't *grow* organically. Someone plans them, surely.'

Tudor leaned forward, elbows on the table, the tea forgotten, and began to explain. His eyes shone with enthusiasm for his subject and affection for small settlements and vernacular houses and farms.

'Take Stockton-on-the-Forest ...' he began.

Angela listened, fascinated. This was a new world to her, completely different to her own field of study which was bounded by the written page. Tudor read from roads and bridges, from the lie of the land and the course of rivers.

Jess came in and up to their table.

'I've been waiting for you,' she said, slightly reproachfully, to Angela.

'Oh, Jess, I am sorry, were we supposed to meet?'

'It is all right,' said Jess, instantly mollified. Everyone can forget. A deliberate slight is quite another matter. 'Hello,

Tudor,' she said, turning her head to include him in the conversation.

Catching his name from Jess, only to forget it two minutes later, Angela said, gathering up her papers, 'Tudor's been enlightening me on his architecture course. It's fascinating.' She smiled brilliantly at him before the two girls walked away.

'*A bientôt,*' said Tudor to her empty chair. He was not dissatisfied with the progress he had made.

This was the first of several similar conversations. Also, two or three times Tudor joined a group which contained Angela. Then he would nod a casual greeting to her as she acknowledged him with a glance, sometimes a smile. From that first moment on he would ignore her and listen intently to the general conversation. She began to think of him as a pleasant part of the scenery.

Bruno Hallam had not proclaimed his allegiance to the game of chess, in fact he had concealed it. He had disliked the desk he was given at Fulford, and one day walking in the centre of York he had noticed one he liked much better, in a shop window. He bought it on the spot and insisted on same day delivery. It was unheard of for police officers to buy their own desks, but somehow the powers-that-be did not like to tackle Bruno about it. They were a little in awe of him. Since his arrival, the planned closure of the staff social club had been put on ice, touch typing had become part of the programme for training, and the new mobile voice-and-data system was being tried out.

So, unreprimanded, Bruno had installed his own desk and kept one drawer in it permanently locked. From time to time staff entering the office unexpectedly had found him gazing into this drawer with an expression of concentration. They all began to wonder what he kept in it.

One day when he was called out to an emergency they found out. A young detective, tiptoeing in with a report, noticed that the mysterious drawer was slightly open, and in a second had found out the secret.

'It is a game,' he announced in the canteen. 'Chess. I've never learned to play it. One of those squared boards like you use for draughts is in the drawer, with the things you play with on it.' He waved his fingers in the air descriptively.

'Men, you idiot,' said his sergeant, who happened to overhear. 'Chessmen. Or "pieces". You never read *Through the Looking-Glass* when you were a child?'

'I didn't read girls' books, sarge.'

'You might have learned something. So! We've got another chess player in the force!'

'You play, then, sarge?'

'I know the rules,' the sergeant said modestly. 'I expect the boss enjoys the chess problems in the newspapers. They are good mental exercise.'

He was one of the few men in the station who did play, and this gave him a great deal of secret satisfaction. From that moment he planned to introduce chess into the conversation with Bruno Hallam when the opportunity arose. It arose the next Monday, when Bruno came into the canteen for a coffee. Moving out of the room with his newspaper under his arm, the sergeant accidentally dropped it on the corner of Bruno Hallam's table.

'Oh! Sorry, sir,' he said, scooping the paper up. He noticed that Bruno had a copy of *The Times* himself—in fact the super was reading it.

'*The Times* is such good value on Monday, isn't it?' went on the sergeant in a polite voice. 'Only 10p!'

'It is good value every day,' responded Bruno without raising his eyes.

'Of course, I buy it mainly for the chess problems,' went on the sergeant.

Then Bruno did glance up briefly.

'They are too easy,' he said, and went on reading the feature which had caught his attention.

The sergeant had never found them too easy. He thought they were difficult. He was about to slink away, when Bruno looked up again, fully at him this time, and said, 'I'll give you a game one lunch-time if you like.'

'Crawler,' someone said to the sergeant

as he left the canteen, walking on air. He glared repressively at the young detective constable who had made the remark.

Pride, they say, goes before a fall. The next day the sergeant lost at chess to Bruno Hallam—not much better than Fool's Mate, unfortunately. Bruno was quite nice about it.

'Chess is a good game for police officers,' he remarked. 'Good training to spot all possibilities. What do you think, sergeant? Should we promote chess in the office? I will issue a challenge. Who knows, we might have a potential Grand Master in the force! Detective Superintendent Hallam challenges all comers to chess Monday lunch-time between the hours of twelve and one. National emergencies, explosions, landslides, or forest fires permitting, of course. I will ask the typist to put up a notice.'

The result was Detective Superintendent Hallam six, other staff nil. Even the young constable, who had spent the weekend learning the game and had bought a little book about unbeatable openings, was wiped off the board in ten moves. Hallam, sometimes merciful though rarely on the chess board, had some pity on the crestfallen constable.

'Practice,' he said, putting a hand on the lad's shoulder. 'That's the only way. Get some of the others to play you. I'll play you again when you've had some more experience. Choose a date next year. Shall we say a year today? All right, that's a promise.'

A chess tournament, proper rules, followed by an exhibition simultaneous game, Detective Superintendent Hallam to meet all comers, was also fixed for a year's time.

And a lot can happen in much less time than that.

12

The new campaign planned by the so-called Ripper began the next day and in due course two weeks afterwards it made the papers, at least the York papers.

Couple scared off sex attacker, read the headline. *'Police in York have praised two people who confronted a sex attacker after hearing his 19-year-old victim's screams for help. A woman in her nightgown and a young man ran to the scene of the late-night attack—and the attacker fled when they faced him. 'If it hadn't been for their timely intervention, I'm sure we would now be investigating an even more serious offence,' said a police spokesman.*

The York University student was attacked as she ran from her residential block towards the Hull road, passing along Windmill Lane, at about 11.15 p.m. on Tuesday. She was Mercy, the girl who had sparred with Angela the night a crowd of women students had stayed up late on the landing, right at the beginning of term.

A man walking in the opposite direction grabbed her by the throat and dragged her into a wooded area between the road and the university's science park before carrying out what police called 'a serious sexual assault'.

He is described as 20 to 25 years old, 5 feet 10 inches tall, with short mousy brown hair and strong build. He was wearing a dark waist-length bomber-type jacket. The attack is the most serious of five on female students in the Windmill Lane area of York over the past two weeks.

Bruno Hallam had taken the press conference.

'The other attacks were not reported to the police,' he said.

It seemed strange to the journalists present that four students had been attacked without a public outcry, but if they were not reported that explained it. The girls had only come forward after hearing about Mercy's experience, and Mercy herself was not available for interview by the media.

Then the police received the letter.

You can't do anything about it, the letter read. *I can take out whoever I like and you can't stop me. Jack the Ripper.*

The four girls who claimed to have been attacked previously were assembled in the police station and being sympathetically interviewed one by one. The word 'claimed' was being used about them because people did strange things, like making allegations which were not true, and even though what they said had the ring of truth about it, it had to be checked out and proved to be as true as the police in fact believed it to be. Jenny Wren and two other women police officers were doing the interviewing; they had been on special courses to help them deal with cases like this.

The attacks had happened at night. The victims were all university students walking home alone down Windmill Lane, in spite of the warnings which had been current in both town and gown for months. All the women had long hair. They described their attacker as wearing either a balaclava or a hat and scarf. He usually came up behind them, dealt them a blow to the head and then put an arm round their neck before trying to drag them off into bushes and undergrowth.

The first victim, a woman aged twenty-three, told how she was hit and grabbed by a man who pulled her backwards with his hands over her mouth. She fell and the man knelt astride her. He said she must do what he wanted or he would kill her, and he ran the blade of a penknife across her arms and neck before tackling the removal of her clothes. Something disturbed him; he got up and pulled her to her feet, she managed to break free and run, but he overtook her and pulled her to the ground again in a garden. By now she had fully regained her powers of resistance—the initial blow had stunned her—and she fought fiercely, finally managing to attract the attention of the people in the house, which scared the man off.

The next attack had been twenty-four hours later, when a nineteen-year-old had been coshed then grabbed in a headlock and dragged into the bushes, but he had not struck her hard enough to make her unconscious and her screams had brought the attention of a boy and his father and their two dogs, and again the man had run off.

The third attack was more to his original pattern. The nineteen-year-old he caught that time was coshed more severely. She fell to the ground, he sat astride her and punched her in the face, reiterating that if she struggled he would kill her. Convinced she was going to die, she listened as if in a nightmare as he streamed insults to women in her ears while he abused her, inflicting several cuts as he tore and ripped at her clothing.

'Why were you walking alone?' asked Jenny.

'I'd been to this night-club,' said the girl, 'and realised I hadn't any money for a taxi and they won't take cheques.'

'I've given a cheque to pay a taxi several

times,' protested Jenny gently.

'They might for *you*,' said the girl. 'They wouldn't for me.'

'Did you actually ask him? I'm sure no reputable taxi-driver would have left a young woman stranded in town by refusing to take a cheque.'

'I didn't ask,' said the girl. 'I thought I had a fiver but when I looked for it it wasn't there. It wasn't raining and I wasn't wearing heels, so I set off to walk. Actually I enjoyed walking until ...' Suddenly reliving the incident, she burst into tears.

And then there was a twenty-five-year-old who had been to the self-defence classes, and she had fought back in a way which must have been very painful for the attacker. What a pity, thought Jenny ironically.

For whatever reasons, none of these four young women had gone to the police.

Then there was Mercy.

It was going to be months before the public heard the full story of Mercy, but Jenny and the other policewoman were hearing her evidence now, feeling sickened at the violence she had suffered. They had travelled to her home to interview her and were sitting next to each other on the settee. Jenny was making notes.

'I can't go back to the uni,' Mercy told them in a choked voice. 'I thought I was going to die. I can't even go out alone, someone has to go with me and it is a real bind for my mum and dad, having to treat me like a baby almost. Sometimes I stay in my room and daren't come out. I was face down,' she said, 'and he was on top of me. His hand was round my face and over my mouth. My nose was pressed into the ground. Grass it was, we weren't in the bushes, we were on the open grass but he had dragged me away from buildings and it was a quiet spot. He had struck me with something hard and heavy, behind the ear. I tried to get free but he was heavy and strong. He was sitting across me.'

'Did he speak to you?' asked Jenny.

'He said, "Shut up or I'll kill you." His voice was sort of husky. Then he said, "If you don't struggle I won't hurt you." He kept saying that. He had gloves on and I thought I was going to suffocate.'

'Did he hit you again?'

'Yes, he punched me. The doctor told you. She examined me.'

'And there was blood—'

'Yes.'

'Your blood—'

'Catch him!' Mercy cried out suddenly. 'Don't let him do it again! I'm always thinking he's going to get me, but if it isn't me it will be someone else. Please ...' Her voice dropped to a whisper and she began to sob. 'Please catch him ...'

Jess and Angela were sitting in Jess's room and drinking coffee from mugs. Jess was eating biscuits. Angela had refused them.

'It is nothing to do with what she was wearing,' Jess insisted.

'Or wasn't wearing,' said Angela. 'What was the story? A woman should be able to walk the streets naked and not be molested? Pull the other one, Jess. That was what Mercy believed. So when she had a quarrel with Beverley she rushes out of our block and goes haring off down the road in a leotard in the middle of winter, which she was wearing because she had been meditating or doing press-ups or whatever daft thing she's into at the moment.'

'You're saying it was her own fault, she asked for it, or something?'

'No, of course I'm not.'

'That's what it sounds like,' said Jess. 'I'm surprised you ever joined the Women's Group at all.'

'I'm surprised myself,' retorted Angela. 'None of you have any common sense.'

'I know what you think. Men respond to stimuli and can't help it, poor things?'

'I'll give you a concrete example,' said Angela. 'You've heard of Dr Priestley?'

'J.B., who wrote *The Good Companions?*'

'No, the eighteenth-century one who discovered oxygen, only one or two other people discovered it at the same time. He invented soda water as well. When he was travelling on the Continent he saw women wearing those backless clogs, you know, I've got a pair I bought in Denmark.'

'So?'

'So he thought it was quite disgusting, showing their heels. Roused erotic thoughts, he said. He wasn't talking about the glimpse of ankle which was something shocking, just *heels*, for heaven's sake. Can you think of anything less sexy than heels? All hard skin, and chilblains in the winter if they were wearing those things?'

'Sometimes I think you like the eighteenth century better than the nineteenth. You should be doing history not Victorian women novelists.'

'All male creatures respond to stimuli and so do female creatures. We may try to drown our impulses under a layer of civilisation but we don't succeed very well. Do you think the peahen doesn't respond to the sight of the cock bird's magnificent eye-bright tail-feathers, when he rattles his quills at her until they sound like a shower of rain? Of course she is thrilled to bits, meek, quiet little creature. And he is responding like mad to the stimulus she's giving him, all that eyes down, dun brown feathers, modest little walk! Like hell! That's just what he wants to be, the big peacock and show her who's boss, but he has to toe the line and court her because that's how he's programmed.'

'You've lost your thread,' said Jess, her anger turning into amusement. 'And you sound terribly young and naïve. Come off it, Ange. What about poor Mercy? You don't seem nearly as sorry for her as you did for Ann Clark.'

'Mercy isn't dead,' Angela said tartly. 'She's lucky. She can pick up her life again, even if it takes her years. Of course I'm sorry, and, Jess, I would never have said anything about how she was dressed, only you brought that whole subject up, let me remind you.'

The police were down on the university like a ton of bricks, examining the security system and talking to the university security men.

'How can we do more than we are doing?' one man asked Bob Southwell, indignantly, over coffee. 'Tell me that, Mr Southwell. We have a public road running through the campus. We have a population of youngsters who are tasting freedom, away from home for the first time. On the whole they are law-abiding but they are up to mischief, not that they see it like that. It is a novelty to them, staying up late if they want to, sleeping under the stars in the summer, eating what they feel like eating when they feel hungry, drinking whatever they can afford, no one to criticise.'

'Tell me ...' Bob said, then hesitated a second. 'Dr Blow. Charming man I thought him. Do you know him?'

'Yes. I know him well. Don't suppose he would know me.'

'What's your opinion?'

'He's a bit deceptive,' the security officer said.

'Deceptive?'

'Appears very charming. Is manipulative.'

'Very charming? To women?'

'That isn't his private opinion, though,' said the security man. 'You should hear what he says about them when there aren't any women there. Go in the Gents when he does and ten to one he'll be effing and blinding about how women should know their place. He speaks really disparagingly, if you want to know. I think he's a control freak.'

'Perhaps you happened to hear him letting off steam on one particular occasion,' Bob said thoughtfully.

'Well ...' said the security man, and gave Bob a significant glance.

They were standing looking through the big windows towards the lake, where the fountain sprang up, trying to meet the dim winter sun. In the distance a few figures jogged along.

'You get many of them?' asked Bob, pointing.

'Yes.'

'Have you any control over the joggers, runners, whatever they are?'

'I told you, this place is freely accessible to the public. It is not a prison. There is a regular jogging route but they don't always stick to it, depends what their aim is. Same with the people who come with dogs. To them it is a nice open space where they can walk through trees and on grass and look at the lake. They aren't doing any wrong, as long as the animals are on a lead and the owners pick up after them.'

Bob Southwell stood silent for a while, watching the joggers in the distance. There was one figure dressed in grey that looked familiar. In fact it looked like Bruno Hallam.

Can't be, Bob said to himself. Not the sort of thing our super would do at all. He is far too sophisticated. If he does any exercise it will be in an expensive gymnasium.

He couldn't quite rid himself though of the thought that Bruno Hallam's home was not far away—hardly more than a quarter of a mile.

Five down, plenty still to go, read the next letter to the police. *Try and catch me, you can't manage it. That description of me was flattering. How she wanted me to be, not how I am, so it won't help you with identification. Don't forget. I can get as many of the filthy sluts as I like. It might be death for them next time, instead of only giving them a scare. I could have killed any one of them. I'll show you how easy it is.*

'What's your impression, Jenny, from these girls?' asked Bob Southwell when Jenny Wren returned to York after visiting Mercy.

'Impression?'

'Yes. I've read your reports. They are fine as far as they go, very factual. What I'm asking you for is impressions, things you can't set down on paper—feelings, intuition. Come on, Jenny. You know what I mean. If you're interrogating someone there's an aura, it isn't only words and movements.'

Jenny was silent for a while, gazing into space. When finally she spoke, she said, 'The impression I get is that this man doesn't like women.'

'That's pretty obvious,' said Southwell.

'Ye-es. What I mean is, he isn't actually attacking them because he wants to be close to a woman, even because he wants to rape. He *doesn't* want to be close. He can hardly bear to touch them, he does not do it in the anger and resentment which can come with sexual attraction. He does it out of loathing.'

'Go on,' said Bob.

'I imagine many rapists rape because they haven't been able to attract a woman in the normal way, or because something about the way a passing woman walks, the way her hair grows, anything, makes their reactions rush up to the surface and dominate them, so they go for her in a kind of madness.'

'Rape is an act of aggression, Jenny.'

'I know, boss. But as I was saying, that isn't how this man works. He plans it, we know from the letters.'

'If they are from him and not a hoax.'

'He plans it to make a point. All the women said he gave them a right earful about the horribleness of their sex, how repulsive their bodies were, how they should realise that they were animals not people and had no right to pretend to be any better than the beasts of the field.'

'Beasts of the field?'

'He seems to have a biblical turn of phrase at times.'

'Rapists often want to degrade their victims,' answered Bob.

'Yes. It is an exaggeration of that side of their behaviour, I suppose.'

'It is a side of men that prostitutes often see.'

'But often it is the men who want—actually want—to be degraded. I don't think a woman ever wants that.'

'Ever, like never, is an absolute and we don't often meet them,' said Bob.

The thing Bob could not forget was that solitary grey figure, jogging along yards apart from the few others doing the same thing. That grey figure that reminded him of his boss, Bruno Hallam. Some words of Linda's came back to him. She had—jokingly, of course—suggested that Hallam had committed that horrific murder in Leeds while he was over there, the time he flew back to York, twenty-five miles, hardly worth hitching a ride on a 'copter for.

Quietly and unobtrusively Bob began to check back on the dates of the attacks over the past months and where Hallam was at the relevant time. Okay, so some of the dates were before Hallam came to York, but Sheffield was only fifty or so miles away, wasn't it? Was he off duty at those times? And if on duty, was he in his office, or off on some vague pursuit which couldn't be checked on?

The biblical-sounding words which Jenny had quoted ... of course the lovely phraseology of the King James Version had entered the language so that anyone might quote it unconsciously; but someone cultured like Hallam was more likely to do so than an uneducated yob, wasn't that true?

Bob wondered who he could confide in. Dave Smart? Linda? Tom Churchyard? They would probably all think he was potty. He had better say nothing and bide his time, being observant.

The next letter made them sit up. Ever since Mercy was attacked the police force had been running special patrols to keep an eye on the university campus.

I've watched your blokes, said the letter. *You are useless. I could have nabbed any girl I wanted any day of the week. All right. I'm going to give you a real challenge. I shall grab a girl and kill her right under your noses on Tuesday the tenth at nine p.m. Be there.*

'Well, Robert,' said Bruno Hallam, putting the sheet of paper down on Bob's desk. It had been to the laboratory for tests and was now encased in a transparent folder. 'What are you going to do about this?'

'Me, sir? I was sure you would be taking over, now this has arrived.'

'Weren't you told you needed more experience, after the selection procedure?'

'Yes.' Bob wondered how on earth Bruno Hallam knew that.

'Right. So get some experience. Meet this challenge. I might be present, I might not. I want you to organise the scene. May I make some suggestions?'

271

'Please do.' Bob was almost speechless.

'Ask for a volunteer from the female members of the force. Surveillance for her, of course. She must be under protection at every second. Study his previous hits and choose the route for her to walk carefully. You may have only moments to rescue her. Floodlights which can be instantly triggered to flood the scene with brilliance. Warn all the women students that there has been a specific threat—without divulging what—and they must not, must not stray around. No one out after dark. We don't want to be watching one place while they are getting attacked somewhere different. On the other hand they must not know the details. The campus will be cold and dark, there might even be a mist. Knowing York as I do after only a few months, I would say there almost certainly will be a mist. All the women students *must* stay inside at the relevant time, *must*. Yet we don't want him to know that this will be the case, though if he's any sense he will expect it. Organise very quietly and discreetly, this directive must not get out.'

In a state of acute nerves for the first time in his life, Bob Southwell confided his thoughts about his boss to his wife, Linda. They were in bed and her thoughts had been on something completely different. She had spent a lot of money on some new perfume. Actually she had bought it when she went off to that christening with the children and had been feeling like treating herself. Going without Bob had been a hassle even though Susan and Paul had loved the train journey, and she had enjoyed the change and meeting her cousin again. It had still been a hassle, dragging the luggage on and off trains, worrying if their packed clothes would have survived uncreased. So she had rewarded herself with a present. She had not used the fragrance since, thinking it was too expensive for every day. Then it occurred to her that it might evaporate if it wasn't used. So she decided to let Bob have the benefit of it, that night.

He never even noticed. In broken

sentences he managed to get out his worry about Hallam, and her hopes and anticipations were forgotten.

'You can't be serious,' she said.

'You suggested it once, yourself, Lindy-lou.'

'I was joking. Bruno Hallam is a bogey-man to you, dearest. You must get rid of the idea for your own peace of mind. He must be all right to have got so far up the ladder in a fairly short time.'

She put all the emphasis on the 'musts'. Bob didn't see any reason why his wife should tell him he 'must' do this and 'must' do that. It was irritating enough when his superior officer did it at work. He withdrew his arm from under her head and shifted slightly away in the bed.

'Why does he go jogging round the uni?' he asked her coldly.

'You aren't even sure that it was him.'

'My sight is pretty good.'

'You do wear glasses, dearest. It isn't perfect or you wouldn't need them.'

'My short-sight problem is completely corrected by the glasses.'

'Of course it is. Don't be huffy. You said you were looking across the lake and the figure you saw was all in grey—tracksuit or something.'

'Yes.'

'You ever seen Hallam in a track-suit?'

'He was also wearing a balaclava. The attacker wears a balaclava.'

'Paul and Susan wear them if it's cold. I've got one in my own drawer, and you have one somewhere. The last time we wore them was taking the children sledging.'

'Hmm,' said Bob. He turned over, and pretended to go to sleep.

Linda got up and made herself a cup of tea.

Try as he might, Bob was not completely able to defeat his irrational suspicion. He lay awake that night turning the matter over in his mind until he thought he would go mad. He tried to distract himself by mentally reviewing the men who were still under suspicion after more than one interview. The ex-con, for instance, convicted for sex crimes with a similar *modus operandi*. He had gone missing, according to the latest check-up. The others had been interviewed again, and search warrants had been obtained. The home of the man who had written on Jenny's windscreen had been searched with damning results, as far as his persecution of Jenny was concerned, but they had discovered nothing to link him with the killing. They still hadn't had time to search the flat of the 'weird' lodger at the newsagent's. Bob thought he must expedite that as soon as possible. As for Dr Blow, research was being done into his CV. Who was the attacker of women, preying on the female half of the population of York?

When morning finally came he had fallen asleep at last.

Knowing he had to get to work, Linda got up and made another cup of tea, carrying the tray upstairs quietly in the hope of not waking the children. It was Saturday, they didn't have to go to school. She and Bob must take this discussion further. As soon as he was sitting up, half awake, managing with a struggle to accept his cup of tea without spilling it, she opened the topic.

'You are being ridiculous about Hallam, Bob,' she said to him.

He was sure she was right. He was at last feeling rational on the subject, but since his confession of the night before he could not refuse to discuss the matter with her.

'Why,' he said to her now, 'why doesn't he want to take over the investigation? Answer me that.'

'You told me he has taken over the public relations bit. You haven't been pleased about losing that bit of glory.'

Looking at his wife, so delectable in her satin dressing-gown flowered in pink and blue shadowy blossoms, with her serene face watching him lovingly, Bob realised that if he had feet of clay—and who hadn't—they were completely visible to Linda. She loved him all the same. He didn't know whether to be proud or humiliated.

'Why choose to live in Heslington?'

'Likes the area, I suppose,' said Linda, shrugging her satin-covered shoulders.

'Why does he go jogging round the university?'

'Needs the exercise to keep fit and the place is handy. Lots of people jog and run there.'

Bob was silent and Linda waited for more reasons for his irrational idea. At last she broke the silence.

'That can't be all. There must be something else that's influencing you.'

'There was the way he reacted to Susan being in the office.'

'A bit unbalanced,' conceded Linda, 'but then, he's a passionate man.'

'Passionate?' Bob looked at his wife more intently. He had thought his superior rather a cold fish.

'Very passionate.'

'In what way?'

'Every way, I should imagine.' Linda laughed at the expression on Bob's face. 'It is very obvious, I think. He controls himself of course. That's the first impression one gets. Great power under immense control, which isn't always easy.'

Bob said nothing, so Linda went on.

'Like a sleeping volcano.'

'Hmm,' said Bob, looking disgusted. 'Something a woman knows, is it?'

These fairly rational, fairly calm conversations, while they alerted Linda to Bob's niggling suspicion, did not completely eradicate it. If only he could understand the man! Southwell thought. If only Hallam was a type he knew and recognised! If only he wasn't so much better off, that didn't help!

The rumour was that Hallam had private means, and it was believable. The confidence that arises from not having to worry about where the next holiday was coming from, or whether the budget would run to a meal out. The casual wearing of fine quality clothes and those very plain, very discreet twenty-two carat cuff links. The faint scent of really good cigars. It did place the man on a different planet, somehow. It was bound to alter his way of thinking, his whole personality. Bob took himself to task. Outer things like this had never influenced his judgement before. 'The rank is but the guinea stamp, a man's a man for a' that' had been his motto. He had always looked for signs of the essential metal of a human being's character and not been distracted by outer signs of cultural differences or of status.

That's it! he thought, now fully alert. I sense in Bruno Hallam some cultural difference and don't know yet of what it consists ...

There was plenty to organise before the deadline the attacker had set them, and it needed meticulous planning. During the next days there were consultations with the university security people; even the Chancellor and the Vice-Chancellor were involved in meetings with the police. One person not involved in them was Dr Keith Blow. The upper echelons of the university staff knew of the accusation his wife had made and while the matter was *sub judice* had hinted politely that his presence was not required.

These meetings were held at various locations without fuss. The feeling that the attacker was watching them and guessing the trap they were preparing for him made everyone ultra-cautious. It was convenient that building works were being carried out at the university for the new computer block. Workmen could be legitimately asked to do various tasks, pile building materials up here or there, making mounds partitioned off with mesh screens, an untidy area within which there could be a police command post.

The police were praying for a cold clear night with a moon and brilliant stars. The attacker was praying for mist and dampness. Lying on a higher slope, evading the patrols, he could watch most of what was happening and plan out his own strategy.

The day before the attack was threatened, news came in from Interpol that Dr Blow had been in prison on the Continent for causing serious bodily harm to his first wife, who, when she recovered, divorced him.

13

Of course all the women students were made aware that there was to be a curfew on their movements, they had to be. As for other women who strayed on to the campus with their dogs, or in their jogging outfits, they had to take their chance. No one thought they were in any danger. University students were what the attacker was now targeting and he seemed to be capable of distinguishing them from other members of the population.

As Tuesday approached Angela became very quiet. A number of things were troubling her. First was the thought that a policewoman was to risk her life for them. A leak of information meant that some of the university women realised that a young policewoman, one with long hair, was going to walk a chosen route in the darkness with every expectation of being struck down. Although safeguards were in place there was a strong likelihood that the attacker would reach her before being apprehended, and as he had said he was going to kill this time, she might well be murdered.

The students hadn't been intended to know what was planned, and most of them didn't. But Tudor Evans' friend Maurice was having an affair with a policewoman and she had been one of those considered for the role of decoy, or bait, however you looked at it. One night when the lovers were in bed the policewoman confided that she had been rejected for the job of doing that lonely walk. Maurice was delighted that she wasn't going to be in danger, appalled that someone else was.

'They might catch him before then, anyway,' his lover said. 'That's what they are hoping, obviously. They're doing all they can to find him. Probably after all the preparations there will be no ambush, or walk, it will be cancelled.'

He didn't know why he told the story to Charles and Tudor, when he joined them on one of their 'site visits'.

'It is completely hush-hush,' Maurice said, worried now that he had revealed the secret. 'You mustn't let on, Tudor. Or you, Charles. If it gets out bang go the police's chance of catching the devil.'

'I won't tell a soul,' said Tudor, adding under his breath, 'except Angela.'

'Jess,' said Angela later, 'come here a minute.'

'What is it?'

'I know you're dashing off to the Star Wars Quiz—isn't it the final tonight?—but there's something I've got to tell you. You know that architectural student who is in Langwith sometimes midday?'

'Do you mean Charles?'

'No, that's not his name.'

'The other one, then, Tudor. Unless it is Maurice.'

'Yes,' said Angela doubtfully. 'Well, Charles is the name of his friend, and Maurice is the third one. Tudor. Funny name—I keep forgetting it. Tudor told me something today.'

'Come on, then. I really have to go off to this quiz.'

'He told me a young long-haired policewoman is going to walk alone through the campus while we are all safe and cosy inside.'

'Oh. That's a bit rotten, isn't it?'

'That's what I thought,' said Angela.

'Very brave of her,' said Jess. 'I wouldn't volunteer for that job. Well, Ange, I'm off.' At which point Jess forgot all about the policewoman. She had her quiz to think about.

Left alone on that Monday night, Angela went to her room and sat looking out of the window. She was endlessly fascinated by the views around the campus and the way they changed, hourly often, with the varying weather. At night, like now, she tried to recognise the stars or the surface contours of the moon. It was one of those brilliant nights that come with frost. Emily Brontë's line came to her mind, 'set with the thickest stars'. Contemplation of the sky, at any time in the twenty-four hours, helped Angela to think. Now she was thinking of the murdered girl Ann Clark and of the soon-to-be-murdered volunteer, a young policewoman with long hair ...

But *we* are being threatened, thought Angela. Not the policewomen. We should be allowed to go out there and risk our lives. We owe it to Ann Clark. Angela felt so close to the unknown Ann that she could almost visualise her, there in the quiet room.

She decided what she must do.

She must show solidarity with Ann Clark; it was being demanded of her.

If evil was threatening the student body, then they must put up their own defence; but as the last thing they should do was sabotage the efforts of the police, any action should be in secret, and—yes—by one person only.

Angela did not see herself as a champion for the women students, or as a female knight in armour. She only knew that it was incumbent upon her to meet as much danger as the policewoman did, in the same way, at the same time. She did not know why this duty had been laid upon her, but it was clear that it had. She knew that she would never rest peacefully again if she shirked what was so plainly her ordained course of action.

'Send not to ask for whom the bell tolls; it tolls for thee.' The bell was tolling for her, for Jess, for Mercy, for the policewoman, for Ann Clark.

And the night was tomorrow night.

Angela went through all the movements of preparing for bed without conscious thought. She liked being on auto-pilot, it left her mind free. She drank her glass of cold milk, cleaned her face, brushed her teeth ...

Her mind was floating free but she had stopped thinking with it. There was no more thinking to do. Only a space of hours to be lived through.

It was the following day. Bob was tense as a bow-string. The light was fading and soon the men would be moving into place. He had planned every position, after studying the lie of the land, as meticulously as if this was a test match and they were his fielders. But this might be a matter of life and death. A girl was to be at risk—one of their own. A miscalculation and she could pay forfeit with her life.

The traffic which thundered along University Road, the spine which provided services for the campus, was beginning to still. It did not need to cease altogether because the bait, the decoy, was to walk along the jogging track.

The temporary police HQ was screened from casual sight. It looked like builders' left-overs, a couple of screens of the kind which prevent the unwary from falling into excavations, a few heaps of blocks.

Through the greyness they could see solitary figures, jogging or running in spite of the coldness and damp. It was a time for solitariness, for the loneliness of the long-distance runner. These men, or they might be women—in their jogging suits who could tell, at least at a distance?—glanced at Bob as he walked quietly around, checking his preparations. There were a few women amongst his officers including the young woman constable, dressed in civvies, who was to do the walk alone.

'You will be well protected,' Bob said to her.

She was to get off a bus at the bottom of the road—a standard service bus but specially commissioned for tonight. It had a few plain-clothes police as passengers, looking as normal as possible. It would stop at the usual place and so the volunteer would come on to the scene from a well-lighted area and walk to begin with on the normal route taken by so many hundred students every day.

'I'm not afraid,' she smiled at him. He could tell that she was tense, ready, excited by the star quality she had suddenly acquired amongst her fellow officers. Her clothing was pale, to show up in the growing darkness.

It was ten minutes to zero when Bob Southwell spotted something familiar about one of the lone joggers, rapidly approaching. As the figure came nearer it was clearly a man, thickset, older than most joggers. Bob knew instinctively by the strong physical reaction he was himself experiencing that this was Bruno Hallam. A frisson ran up Southwell's spine leaving his body alert and tense, the fine short hairs on arms and legs feeling as if they were standing out from his flesh, his chest expanded full of oxygen, his eyes newly able to pierce the darkness.

'Come with me,' Southwell muttered to two of his men. His alertness infected them. Without a word they followed at his heels. They ran lightly to intercept the man. They stopped in front of him.

'Sir,' Southwell said simply, as he confronted his superior officer. Hallam stood still. He was wearing a grey jogging suit, and a grey balaclava on his head.

'I don't know why you are here, sir, in this unofficial capacity, just when we're about to start this operation. You knew it was going to happen.'

Bob waited for Hallam to explain himself.

Bruno Hallam said nothing, so Bob Southwell went on.

'All the way through this case I had been uneasy about some of your actions, and would be grateful if you would just stay here quietly and let us get on with this.'

Behind him the two other detectives stiffened in astonishment. This couldn't be happening. But their detective superintendent stood still and said nothing. Bob went on, 'You will understand why I now ask you to remain in the company of these officers while this operation takes place. Having you jogging in the area might endanger the whole thing. You may already have ruined everything. The murderer may be witnessing this confrontation.'

It was a confirmation of Southwell's unease that Bruno Hallam still said nothing. He allowed himself to be escorted by the two men to the concealed head-quarters. There, the detective constables stood one on either side of him. Everyone was standing quite motionless. Around them the night, in contrast to the night before, was black darkness and visibility was very poor. Without being misty exactly, the air was thick with dark and the sky was dark, no sign of moon, no Pole Star, no Orion's Belt, no Dog Star faithfully following at the heels of his master through the aeons, no Venus, only black night above them. They were so quiet that a deep breath would have seemed like an outrage in the silence.

The bus pulled up at the bus-stop and WPC Davies got out and set off on her solitary walk.

She passed the houses and the street lamps and at last reached the unlit desert of her planned path.

They were all so intent on following her approach through the darkness with straining eyes and ears alert for the slightest hostile movement towards her, that a girl much nearer to them escaped their notice. The girl, standing hidden from their view, did not move. She was wearing a long dark rainproof and its hood was over her head, her hands in its pockets.

WPC Davies' pale three-quarter-length coat and swinging white handbag pin-pointed her movements. She walked casually as though she had all the time in the world and was enjoying the evening air. She passed the silent hidden policemen.

The other police, scattered strategically over the area, held their breath as they marked her progress.

The pale figure gradually receded. Bob Southwell strained his eyes to catch the last glimpse. Now it was out of his hands. He must rely on the girl herself and the watchers out there. Heartbeat by heartbeat he waited.

The other girl dropped the rainproof to the ground and stepped quietly across rough grass to join the route the police-woman had taken. Bob, gazing in the other direction, did not realise her presence until she walked right past the command post. He could do nothing. To burst out and stop this stupid student's walk would have blown WPC Davies' cover. Everyone in the command post realised this. Everyone out in the field realised this. The whole operation had been put in jeopardy and there was nothing they could do about it.

She was a tall slim girl, wearing clothing that looked more suitable for a summer than a winter's night. A short, sparkling white T-shirt, sleeveless, showed a bare midriff, and shorts left most of her long legs bare. Over one arm she carried a folded light-coloured track-suit. On her feet were white trainers and even in the darkness her long blonde hair seemed to catch stray gleams of light.

Angela walked with her usual graceful stride, nonchalantly taking the same route the other girl had walked seconds before. Ahead of her but only barely discernible, WPC Davies was already well along the planned route.

As the tall blonde girl walked past them the two officers with Bruno Hallam felt him tense. They thought he was going to break away from their informal custody and one of them laid a hand lightly on his arm. Bruno, staring, straining his sight after the girl, did not seem to be aware of this. The two detectives were uncomfortable. Hallam was a god-like figure to them, someone so far above them in the pecking order that the idea of holding him in any kind of restraint seemed a presumption on their part which he might later resent and avenge. But for this night's duty they were in Southwell's command, and acting on his orders. If anyone's job was on the line, his was. Strangely, too, Hallam had still not said a word of protest. The sight of the tall blonde girl had changed him. They could sense that clearly without the use of words.

The policewoman walked on, oblivious of the rival temptress behind her. There were two hundred yards between them. Together but apart they moved in the night. WPC Davies passed on without incident. She reached the end of her planned route safely.

It was as Angela moved out of sight that the attack happened, and to some of the watchers it was not clear which of the girls had been the victim. There was a moment's scuffle and a scream.

In that instant everyone in the command post forgot Hallam and the strangeness of Bob's behaviour to him. They expected the hidden policemen to rush in. Their hard-worked eyes had made out a pale shape falling to the ground and now an indistinct figure bent over her. Someone touched a switch and the floodlights burned like daylight, harshly illuminating every grass blade. The men out there began to run from their places, towards the two on the jogging route. In the blink of an eye it was clear that it was the second girl who lay under repeated blows on the ground.

Bob Southwell was never to forget the great howling cry which broke from Bruno Hallam, seeming to fill the sky as the superintendent burst forward, away from his captors, through the camouflage of the command post and towards the fallen girl. It was a wordless shout of such intense emotion that it could never be forgotten, like a great roar from a lion in the night. Then, as the man ran desperately forward, arms outstretched, stumbling over the rough ground in his haste, he shouted out again, a single word so incongruous that Bob could hardly believe his ears, a word so strange and unexpected that everyone was momentarily frozen still.

What Bruno Hallam shouted was, 'Munchkin!'

14

When the police floodlights snapped on, the scene was bright as day.

Angela could only think that she was not going to give in. Even after the lights came on, the third blow, which was already descending, did not pause but came crashing down on her skull, knocking her sideways on the ground. She moaned and dug her fingers into the grass. She hadn't realised it would hurt so much. She was not going to give in, but she thought she was going to die. The pain was incredible. The feeling of the cold ground was grim, unyielding, giving her no shelter.

There had been no sound from the attacker. She had hoped for an instant's warning but there had been none. A picture had come into her mind together with the first crash of pain, a picture of Ann Clark's dead face—a milli-second flash of vision as she fell out of her own control to the ground. She had lifted her head then, defiantly, and the vision was gone as the second blow descended. Because she had lifted her head, the impact of the second blow was higher on her skull than the attacker had meant. Her head was thrust to the ground by the weight of the cosh. Blood from her scalp ran down her face, blinding her.

The lights blazed on before the third blow, but it came down, finishing its arc. Knocked sideways, she now lay helpless waiting to be finished off.

A sound seemed to fill her ears like the whisper from a sea shell. It was an insidious sound, which wound its way down her external auditory canals to vibrate her eardrums and then be passed by the hammer bones, the anvil bones and the stirrup bones to the oval windows of the fluid-filled shell-shaped cochleas and thence through her acoustic nerves to her brain. Once there the battered brain had to understand it. Even after that, she had to realise how to react to what her senses were telling her. Cold and pain extended her time scale. Seconds seemed like centuries. She was more tired than after the most fraught hurdle race, more lost than a babe in the wood.

It was an unbelievable sound, anyway. A sound she had not heard for many years except in her dreams. She moved her hand against the grass. There were other sounds but she only heard one, the one which came again, closer, louder in her ears. *Munchkin*. It had never sounded desperate before.

Somehow Angela raised herself to her knees. Bob Southwell could see her face, framed with long blonde hair, a flood of blood down from the hair, over her features. Her lips seemed to move, and he thought she was mouthing the word, *Daddy*.

Bob Southwell was running, everyone was running, the details of the scene coming ever closer.

Several policemen were gripping the weird man who lived over the newsagent's shop and dragging him away from the fallen girl. Knowing he would not escape, everyone else was focusing on Angela. Between Bob Southwell and Angela was Bruno Hallam, well ahead, running with all his strength, and as he ran his voice was raised once again, this time shouting, 'Angela!'

Bruno Hallam reached her. He fell on his knees and most tenderly gathered the girl into his arms. He eased her head on to his shoulder, murmuring, 'Oh, Angela, little one.'

Angela tried to speak to him, but although his name formed on her lips she could not make a sound. Instead slow tears ran from her eyes to soak the shoulder of his grey tracksuit.

They were in a different world.

'Daddy, oh, Daddy,' was all she wanted to say. The feeling of safety after danger was overwhelming. The physical pain she was enduring and the emotional release and sense of wonderful serenity of spirit were almost more than she could bear. Dizziness swept over her and for the first time in her life she fainted.

For a few awful moments her father thought he had lost her. She lay slumped in his arms, her blood pumping over him.

'Oh no, my daughter!' he gasped. 'Oh no!'

Before he could turn to ask for help she murmured something wordless and he felt her eyelids flutter against his cheek.

The outpost policemen, who had run up next after the attacker was captured, stood around not knowing what to do. Southwell reached the group. He did not even glance at the captured man, who was being marched off by several sturdy policemen.

Everyone's eyes were on the girl and her father, realising that they were witnessing moments which for Hallam and Angela were transcendental. No one said a word. For what seemed like minutes they stood without moving, watching.

At last Hallam turned his head towards them.

'Give me a hand here,' he said, and his voice was a new voice they had never heard before.

'The paramedics are ready, sir,' Bob Southwell said respectfully. 'We have an ambulance waiting.'

'Your hand, Bob,' Hallam said more firmly. 'Under my left armpit. Mr Smart, you help Angela. Gently, mind. I've got hold of her but she may need more help.'

Bruno Hallam scrambled to his feet still holding Angela and helping the girl to rise from her knees. They stood, with him still cradling her in his arms. She was almost as tall as he was, but she was collapsed against him.

Then, turning to Bob Southwell again, Bruno Hallam said, 'Bob, this is my daughter. For ten years we have not met, until now.'

'Sir,' said Robert Southwell, 'I didn't understand. I am sorry.'

'How could you understand? I'm not blaming you.'

Bruno's voice was still changed. No longer a roar, it was gentle. 'Please get that ambulance,' he went on. 'I'm taking her down to the hospital.'

The ambulance drove up, over grass

302

and gravel. The paramedics were anxious to take over from Hallam, but he was oblivious of them.

'Come on, my dear,' he said. He supported Angela, who had begun to weep. Gently he eased her up the steps, the paramedics assisting. They all went into the ambulance and Bruno Hallam and Angela sat together. Southwell, escorting them, saw them settled, her head on his shoulder and his cheek on her hair, one arm round her shoulders, his other hand holding hers.

Bob heard Angela say softly, 'Oh, Daddy, I've missed you.'

'Not more than I've missed you,' Hallam answered, and his voice, low and loving, made Bob Southwell feel he was intruding.

Bob backed out, saying to the ambulance staff, 'Don't disturb their privacy. She will be all right till you get to the hospital.' He closed the door on them. With a police car in attendance, the ambulance drove away.

As he stood there, alone in the glare of the floodlights, watching the retreating ambulance, Bob wondered how it would feel not to meet his daughter Susan for ten years. He was filled with a wave of protective love for Susan which surprised him by its strength. He had seen Susan born, lived family life with her daily since, but not until this moment had he realised how much she meant to him. It was as if Linda stood aside and for once he could see his daughter clearly. Not to see Susan for ten years! To stand by and hear her attacked, hear her scream! He wondered at Bruno Hallam's restraint. Even when he, his inferior in the force, semi-arrested him, Hallam had not protested.

When they reached the hospital emergency department the team there were ready to examine Angela's wounds, but she clung to her father and refused to be parted from him.

'Come on,' he said tenderly. 'They have their work to do. I won't leave. Let them do their best to help.'

She still clung to his hand as much of her hair was snipped away and her scalp examined. The blood was wiped from her face.

'X-ray first,' said the doctor. 'Then I'm afraid there will have to be stitches. We'll put on a temporary dressing in case there is any delay, I see you are still bleeding a little. We'll wheel you to X-ray and your father can come and wait for you outside. How are you feeling?'

'Dazed,' said Angela faintly. It was a struggle to speak. 'And my head hurts. I hurt all over.'

'We will examine you in case you've broken anything, but I'm reasonably confident that we'll find it is only bruising, apart from your head,' said the young doctor in a reassuring voice.

Angela seemed pleased but Hallam took this reassurance with a pinch of salt. His hand, large, warm and strong, closed tightly over hers.

'There will be some trauma,' the doctor said in an aside to Hallam. 'We would prefer to keep her in overnight, but you can sit up with her if you wish. Once she is home, don't hesitate to ask if she needs psychiatric help, or if either of you needs counselling.'

'I think the thing we need most at the moment is some hot sweet coffee,' said Hallam. 'Hot as hell, black as night, and strong as love.'

Angela smiled from the hospital trolley. This was a familiar description from her childhood. Many times she had heard her father express his wish for coffee and always he said, 'Hot as hell, dark as night and strong as love.'

'There are coffee machines,' one of the nurses said. 'Anyone will show you where the nearest is.'

'Let's hope it is not like one hospital where I had to visit the emergency ward after my aunt had a fall,' said Hallam, 'and there were no cups in any of the machines.'

The nurse assured him rather coldly that in this hospital, at this moment, they had plenty of cups.

The escorting police car had been parked and DI Dave Smart now appeared in Emergency.

'Is there anything I can do, sir?' he asked.

'Yes. First you can get us both a hot sweet coffee, if you wouldn't mind, David. Then you will want a statement. Come up with us and Angela can give it in the intervals of waiting. I think she will be able to talk now. There is always waiting in hospitals unless they are trying to resuscitate somebody. It will save time later, you will be able to get straight on with things. I will give a statement too, keep my mind off whatever is happening to my daughter. They will make me stay outside. Will you tell Mr Southwell, David, that I am taking a day's leave tomorrow?'

Later, Hallam said, 'They are keeping her in overnight and I am staying with her. There will be no need to disturb us with police business, tell Mr Southwell. Have you got an official car here with someone to send?'

'Two of them, boss,' said Dave Smart.

'Here are my car keys and the garage key. Ask them to fetch my car down from home, would you? When the powers that be let me take my daughter home I will need it.'

She overheard them.

'Home!' said Angela. 'Home!' and she began to cry again. She was in a strange state between exaltation and misery. She had been keyed up to her ordeal, feeling fellowship with that other girl, equally without family, equally unprotected. Choosing to put herself in a position of danger had been to express solidarity with the oppressed. By dressing as she did on a night when cords and jumpers would be more appropriate she was carrying out the feminist dictum that a woman should be safe in any place whatever she chose to wear—or not to wear.

It had been horrible. She had expected to see the man and wrestle with him. The blow had taken her by surprise and in her wrought-up state the shock was the more terrific. Then, lying on the ground in pain—expecting further blows and realising the whole thing might go horribly wrong and she might die, lying there on the grass—at that very moment, her father's voice ... the voice she had given up hope of ever hearing again. The touch of him, the protection of his arms, the scent of his clothing, had come as they had so often come to her when she had been a little child, when pain or some small childish trouble had overwhelmed her world. A fragment of a forgotten hymn came to her mind. It did not mean human fathers, of course. They were only human, only fallible, but sometimes, on occasion, they could also stretch forth strong arms and offer safety.

WPC Davies was there in the hospital, hoping to be useful and behaving very well, all things considered. She had expected to be the heroine of the hour, and then this civilian had stolen her thunder and put herself in danger unnecessarily! Luckily Marion Davies was a compassionate girl, her heart was moved by the reunion of father and daughter, and she cheered herself up by remembering that she had escaped several nasty blows on the head.

'I think I'll be better soon,' said Angela.

She was in hospital for twenty hours, and in that time Bruno Hallam was constantly at her bedside. She was supposed to keep quiet but he talked, catching up with the events of ten years.

'Why, Daddy?' asked Angela. It was two days before she stopped using the childish name. 'Why did you and Mum split up?'

He explained that he had been a hardworking young copper at the time, and her mother had not enjoyed being the wife of someone who worked unsocial hours, and whose job made them pariahs in their community.

'You could have gone on seeing me.'

He took a deep breath. 'The last time I saw you you looked at me as though you hated me,' he said. 'I didn't want that to be a long-term attitude. It was better not to see you at all.'

Angela wept when he told her that, although she had not seen him, he had been keeping an eye on her and trying to ensure her safety, year by year.

'If I'd known ... it would have been so much easier,' she said. 'I thought—Mother said—you had forgotten you had a daughter.'

The tests showed that Angela's skull had not suffered permanent injury, though she was developing king-size swellings. After careful consideration the medical staff decided Bruno Hallam could take her home. He had communicated briefly with her mother and stepfather, soothed their fears, and arranged to keep them in the picture about her recovery.

When she was released, in the early evening of the following day, Hallam drove his car to the front entrance of the hospital and, moving weakly, Angela got into it. Then father and daughter went together to collect whatever she needed from her room on campus.

As they set off Angela said, 'This car has the same feel your cars always had, Dad.'

Her childhood came flooding back to her. All the times when she had ridden in the back and her parents in the front, she listening, usually, to her mother complaining about something. The times—more precious—when she had been dropped off at school or ballet class by her father and sat in the front passenger seat on the journey, feeling very grown up.

'I've had several different cars in the ten years,' he said.

'Your cars are all alike. They all have that feeling of solidity and comfort, and move smoothly, and smell a little of your cigars.'

'I like safe cars,' he answered. 'Not that there is such a thing.'

Once in Bruno's house Angela burst into tears.

'Daddy,' she said, and clung to him. 'It's been awful, you can't think how awful. I've missed you every single day.'

'Do you think I haven't missed you, little one?' he said gently. Holding her at arm's length, he went on, 'Not that you are my little girl any longer, Angela, even though, back there, there didn't seem to be any change between us.'

'Five foot nine, is that what you mean?' and she smiled through the tears.

'Nearly as tall as me. Did you really think I had lost sight of you? Why do you think I applied for a job in York when I

312

knew you were going to be here?'

'But I didn't know where you were or what you were applying for,' she pointed out.

'Why do you think I took up jogging at my age and with my figure, if not to keep an eye on your welfare? But we have gone over this, off and on, a dozen times since last night.' His rueful expression coaxed another smile from her.

'I shall never be tired of hearing how you kept an eye on me,' she said. 'But jogging—did you? Is that why you've got on that funny get-up?' She looked doubtfully at his jogging suit, which he was still wearing although it was stained by her tears and blood.

'Criticising already!' he said. 'I'm going to warm this soup and you are going to eat a bowlful and then go to bed.'

She sat at the kitchen table and looked around her. 'This looks like home. That's our kitchen cabinet.'

'And tastes like home, I hope.' He put a bowl of steaming soup in front of her and then served one for himself.

'This is your great-grandmother's recipe. When I was young it never failed to comfort me.'

'You've got all the old furniture and pictures,' she said. 'I noticed as we came through.'

'You always were too observant for your own good. Your mother didn't want anything, she wanted all new stuff. It was from my grandparents anyway, though if she had liked it and wanted it I would have shared. But being half Scandinavian she always preferred that kind of furnishing.'

'I thought our house contents had all gone to a saleroom.'

'Well, they didn't. Eat your soup.'

'I've been so unhappy,' said Angela. 'Why didn't you have me with you?'

'You know perfectly well your mother got custody.'

'And I had to live with her and that awful Raoul.'

'Awful is a childish exaggeration,' he said firmly, 'and his real name is Frank. I'm sure your stepfather was perfectly kind to you.'

'I don't want to talk about those years,' she said.

'Neither do I. Eat your soup. There is some more in the pan. But we will have to talk them through, Angela. Not tonight. You are sounding like my little girl again but we've got to ...' He felt he ought to sound a warning bell, to remind her that they would have to create a new, different relationship, then his resolve melted. Let us, he thought, be back again ten years, just for a while, as long as she needs to relive that childishness and dependence. We need to allow ourselves to show our feelings.

Instinctively the father realised that Angela had reached a point beyond which she could not, emotionally, grow. She needed to talk through her desolation and longing, to be comforted, then finally to be able to see him as a whole man complete with his faults. Then she could scold him for those faults, lose her temper with him perhaps. There was also the trauma of the attack to get over, before she was ready to take on the world, to be an adult in earnest.

Aloud he said, 'Somehow I knew last night would be crucial, even though you amazed me with what you did. I couldn't believe it when I saw you walking past the command post. Whatever strange fore-knowledge I had, it made me spend yesterday afternoon making this soup.'

'You don't know how good it tastes,' she said, spooning up the last from her second bowlful. 'Is there any more?'

'That's enough for tonight. Come into the sitting-room.'

In the sitting-room she once again burst into tears, looking round at familiar items of furniture, but soon stopped, and they talked for an hour before Bruno Hallam said, 'You look too tired to talk any more, pet. I'll show you where the bathroom is ... That pink towel is for guests, use that ... Here's your sponge bag ... The spare bed is made up and aired. You go to sleep, Angie. I'm going to sit up for a while. Gute Nacht, schlaf gut, as Grandma used to say.'

After a quick hug and kiss he went downstairs again.

Angela realised she was immensely tired. It was only her father's authority which ensured that she cleaned her teeth and rinsed her face with cold water. As she undressed and slid into bed she looked round and thought again of the home of her childhood. The colour of the walls was the same she had once had, long ago. The pictures had hung in her grandmother's house. The embroidered pillowcases had been her grandmother's also. The books by the bed, with familiar titles and bindings, were ones her father had had as long as she could remember, which she had often pulled from his bookshelves and struggled to understand. Happily, she slept.

15

When Angela and her reunited father drove off in the ambulance, Bob Southwell was left holding the baby, or in this case the murderer, and with the whole unwrapping of the series of attacks still before him.

He turned away from the road as the distant ambulance rounded the bend into Field Lane. Walking back to the command post he dragged his mind from the subject of fathers and daughters and focused it on the captured man. In his absorption with Bruno and Angela he had not even noticed who they had captured.

Sergeant Diamond met Bob as he walked.

'We've sent Sonny down to HQ,' he said.

'Good. Best place for him. I'd better get down there. What do we know about him so far?'

'Quite a lot actually, sir. He is one of the suspects we've been interviewing. We know his name and address for a start. He's unmarried, lives alone.'

'Dr Blow? No, he's married. Is it that vagrant, Spendlove?'

'He went missing, sir.'

'I know.'

'We have circulated other forces, trying to find out Spendlove's whereabouts, as you know, sir. But the man we've caught isn't him.'

'This isn't a guessing game, Terry. Just tell me who the hell we caught.'

'The weird one,' said Sergeant Diamond. 'The one who lives over the newsagent's shop.'

'We've got a search warrant for his home. It hasn't been put into effect yet, has it?'

'No, sir. We've been frantically busy since the attacker started sending letters and going for students. Other things took priority. We put it off.'

'Find that warrant, Terry. I don't care what time it is. And when you've got it, bring it to me. I'll be at Fulford. I want to look at his den before anyone else does. Quietly and on my own.'

Terry Diamond knew his Southwell. He knew Bob's liking for visiting the scene of a crime, and standing silently absorbing the atmosphere. It seemed to clarify his thoughts and often got results which would have taken longer to arrive at any other way. But he had never before known his boss to visit a criminal's home in this fashion.

Southwell was speaking again.

'Terry, can I leave you blokes to finish up here?'

'You certainly can, sir.'

'Right. See you later. As soon as you've got that warrant, I'll visit his pad. Progress meeting after breakfast in the canteen.'

By the time Bob reached HQ the prisoner had gone through the basic procedure of admittance and the long coils of the British legal system were already winding round him.

At 5 a.m. Southwell was standing outside

a suburban shop hardly a mile from the university. Mornings always seemed grey, over this newsagent's shop. The bright and airy university campus was a different world to this place, so near geographically. It was hard to define the source of its sleaze, for it was clean enough, although the dogs cocked their legs on the corner of the brickwork on either side of the door, and the traffic of many feet meant that the floor, washed every morning at six, was filthy again by closing time twelve hours later.

Bob knew already that the lodger, the attacker, lived in one of the rooms over the shop, with use of kitchen and bath.

A van arrived and dumped bundles of newspapers on the doorstep. A minute later a car, rather an old one, drew up and the owner got out.

'You the police?' he asked Southwell.

'We spoke earlier, Mr Kelly,' replied Bob.

'About the lodger, right?'

'Yes.'

'What are you wanting to do?'

'I'd like to talk to you first, if I may. Then, as you know, we have a search warrant. Before the team arrives to go over the place I would like to take a look.'

'Feel free. I've got the newspapers to mark up,' said Jack Kelly. 'If you can talk or listen while I'm doing them, you're welcome.'

They went down the passageway at the side of the shop and through a door which led into a small hallway with a work surface on one side. The side door was shut behind them. Then the newsagent walked through the shop and brought the bundles of newspapers and magazines through. In the hallway Jack Kelly spent the first working hour of his day marking up the papers into rounds, ready for the news-girls and -boys to collect and deliver as soon as possible after six o'clock.

As he began to sort things out, Bob Southwell leaned against the wall near him and asked, 'Describe your lodger to me, Mr Kelly.'

His head bowed over the job, Kelly

answered, 'The name is Jack, Mr Police-man.'

'Bob,' said DCI Southwell.

'Bob. My lodger is a youngish man between twenty and thirty. A thin, insignificant individual, without a job. He seems to manage, with the aid of the state. I expect his needs are few. The customers in the shop hardly notice him although he scurries through quite often, clutching a few items of food.'

'Is he a good customer in your own shop?'

'No. He is a dead loss. We sell newspapers, magazines, cigarettes, sweets, greeting cards, fancy ornaments and sewing cotton. He doesn't buy any of those things.'

'What do your assistants think about him? You did say you had two assistants, didn't you, Jack?'

All the time Jack Kelly was automatically marking up papers and putting them into rounds as he did so. Each round went into a delivery bag. There was obviously an order to it, even to the way the bags were placed by the side of the door.

'If the assistants think about him at all,' said Jack, 'they must assume he lives on baked beans, potatoes, carrots, white sliced bread, and tinned meat. And they would be right.'

Bob Southwell decided not to reveal that one of the assistants had provided information to the police, accusing the lodger of being the attacker. Instead he said, 'Okay for me to mooch about outside?'

'Mooch as much as you like.'

It was still dark, though a large moon sailed in the sky, presently to be dimmed by the dawn.

At the back of the shop was a yard with coal bunkers, where coal still lay, unused since the Clean Air Act outlawed it. Then there was a garage with a loft over. The owner had already told Bob that he parked his car in the garage occasionally if he came for the whole day. It also housed the lodger's moped. Neither vehicle was there on this particular morning. The car was parked at the front of the shop, causing no obstruction at so early an hour, and the moped, which had been found on the campus, was in police custody.

No one used the loft. In the manner of unused places it had accumulated its own private belongings of wood and metal and old upholstery. No one but the loft itself knew from whence they came. No one owned them, but in that place with dim light through unwashed windows they could decay and softly gather dust to themselves, and the mice could scurry over them.

Bob went up the ladder, put his head over the edge of the loft floor, saw the thick dust everywhere, and withdrew. Next he spent some minutes, quarter of an hour, perhaps even longer, exploring the garage and yard. By the time he went back through the side door into the hallway, the first newsboy had arrived. Within a few minutes, the space was filled with jostling, chattering children. Jack ignored them as he ignored Bob's re-entry, but now and then he passed over a satchel filled with papers and magazines to the right child for a delivery round.

Bob went past the busy newsagent and the chattering children—who fell suddenly quiet—and climbed the narrow stair.

Upstairs, he thought about the lodger, presumably still asleep at five o'clock on most mornings, being woken by the thump, thump, of the bundles of newspapers and magazines arriving on the front doorstep between the dogs' two urinating places. Then the light in the hallway behind the shop would go on. The owner would drag the newspapers through the shop and begin his marking up, the first cigarette of the day between his lips.

The lodger upstairs would lie listening to the sounds which had grown familiar. Later, when one by one the children arrived at the side door, there would be the talk in their high clear voices, with the deeper tones of the owner, speaking through his cigarette, giving them instructions.

At six o'clock the first assistant arrived, and even as the thought crossed his mind Bob Southwell heard the click of the shop light, heard the woman rattle up the blind on the door, and a few minutes later heard her set to, washing the floor.

He went downstairs again and glimpsed her through the door from the hallway into shop. She was a shapeless bundle of a woman in her fifties. Her knees seemed to be hurting her as she moved backwards over the red tiled floor with her bucket, and by the time she ended by washing the shop step and rinsing down the two doorposts her hands were red and raw.

Bob Southwell retreated out of sight again and paused halfway up the stairs.

For the first half-hour there were few customers. Those who did come were regulars who only took a moment to serve. A *Mirror* and a packet of Rothmans. A *Sun* and an ounce of St Bruno. A *Telegraph* and a packet of mints. The second assistant arrived at half-past six, younger, even at this time in the morning wearing make-up with eye shadow and scarlet lipstick, and scent so overpowering it could be detected by Bob on the stairs, even through the smells of newsprint, tobacco and confectionery. She hung up her coat in the store cupboard where the cigarettes, tobacco and sweets filled the shelves. Bob caught a glimpse of the back of her head, and saw her hand reach out for her nylon overall trimmed with white.

The lodger, drowsing still in bed, not yet ready to get up, would have heard the sharp ting of the shop doorbell and the footsteps and grunted greetings. The assistants knew these men by their purchases. Bob, now, could hear the women's conversation.

'Has Twenty Bensons been in yet?' asked the younger of the two.

'Haven't seen him,' said the older, fat, sloppy-looking woman.

'Jack might have served him. Only I was saving this mag for him, that's all.'

'Jack might have served him,' agreed the older woman.

Jack, having sent the last of the paper-boys and girls on their way, was now enjoying a quiet cigarette in the back room which had once been a family dining-room.

Bob put himself in the lodger's place. He might well have stood silently on the turn of the stairs, listening to the conversation before going into the bathroom to wash. Remembering the messages the police had received, Bob imagined the man feeling dislike rising in his throat. The conversation which Bob found amusing he would have found, perhaps ...

'Puerile. Female,' the man was to say later that day. 'Speaking cheekily of their betters. Didn't they know they were nowts, nothings in the scheme of things, chattels to be done with as men liked, not worth the vote ...'

'You think they shouldn't have the vote?' Bob was to ask. Obviously the man particularly resented the fact that women had gained the franchise, all those years ago before he was born. Strange.

'Politicians give into them, court their votes, let them imagine they have power. They should only have the power of dogs or swine, in other words none.'

'Is it really the assistants in the shop you are talking about?' Bob was to ask, and the man would explain that it was torment to him to hear these voices in which there was no trace of submission and none of the refinement which he thought he wished for, but would in fact have resented as much as the coarse speech.

But that was to come later. At this early morning moment, Jack threw his stub into the hearth and walked through into the shop.

'Make a cuppa, Kim, will you,' he said. 'See if that copper wants one as well while you're at it. I'll wait on here for a bit, have a crack with the lads.'

The working men of the area, stopping off at the shop on their way to their jobs, came as much for those morning words with the owner as for the goods they bought. That and the bit of flirtation they enjoyed with the two women.

The shop bell rang as the door swung open. In a few minutes the ringing would be almost continuous as the morning rush got under way.

Eileen served Twenty Bensons and passed him the magazine Kim had put by for him.

Jack served *Mirror* and Polos, who stayed

330

a couple of minutes telling a bit of gossip.

Kim came back with the mugs of tea and served *Telegraph* and a Benn's Bar.

'I'll have a Kit-Kat as well this morning, Flower,' said *Mail* and a Tin of Snuff.

Flower was Kim, who smiled coyly at him.

'He's getting as bad as *Times* and Fisherman's Friend,' said Jack, teasing her, when *Mail* and a Tin of Snuff had gone.

'Well, I can't help it if I'm attractive, can I?' asked Kim, putting on her best smile for *Sun* and Chewing-gum who had just walked in.

'What's that?' asked the customer.

'Kim flirting again,' said Jack.

'She can have me any time she likes,' said *Sun* and Chewing-gum, giving her a leer.

'You are awful,' said Kim.

Bob, on the landing, drank the mug of hot tea Kim had brought to him.

'I was in your home earlier today,' Bob was to say to the man.

'On that landing? Listening to those

whores in the shop? They make me want to puke. None of the customers know how to handle women. Treat them as if they were human beings. They are Things. Sub-human. Put on earth only to make men be filthy with them. Even the old ones. Even Eileen, whose great breasts hang down to her waist and whose stomach has risen to meet them. I have to go into the bathroom to try to get the taste of their voices out of my mouth, to cleanse my body and mind with the cold water which is usually all that is on offer in that dump.'

Bob went into the bed-sit and looked round. The lodger must have often whiled away the hours sitting aimlessly on the bed. Opposite, stuck on the wall, was an enlarged copy of an advertisement from a magazine. The top half of a woman, elegantly dressed, hair immaculate, jewelled, sophisticated. At waist level her image stopped as if she was the magician's lady cut in half. Joined at the waist, a mirror image below showed her naked, without ornament, hair loose and flowing.

One thing Bob was never going to know

was that the lodger had once seen an upside-down doll, in fact he had a remote infant memory of having possessed one. One way up it was a pretty girl but turn it the other way up, invert the wide skirt over its head, and it was a witch. They were clever dolls. The maker had fun finding new combinations of opposites. She would have been sorry to know of the fate of the girl/witch doll. It had been stabbed with the kitchen scissors, stamped on, urinated on, defecated on, and its two heads had, in turn, been squashed in the jamb of the door. When it was reduced to a wet, muddy, foul lump it was thrown into the dustbin. Potato peelings and left-over cabbage covered it.

'Where is that nice dolly the lady gave you?' the infant was asked. He could not speak well enough to say. He shook his head, indicating ignorance.

'You are always losing things,' he was scolded. He looked up with a depth of hate behind the innocent gaze ...

Bob stood and wondered what product the advertisement had been selling; it did not in itself evoke anything, perfume, hair spray, fast cars or expensive chocolates. It existed as an image only, presumably a focus for the weird man's campaign of hate.

Bob felt he had seen enough. He had been careful not to touch anything, advancing only a few paces into the room and standing still in contemplation. No doubt the team who was coming later that day to examine the place for evidence would have all kinds of finds and conclusions, but he himself had had enough. He was full of the longing to get away. The council estate surrounded and overwhelmed him. It seemed to clog the air he breathed.

Bob had the prisoner brought into an interview room and settled down with DC Jenny Wren in attendance. The tape recorder was running according to the rules.

For a few minutes (it only seemed like hours to the prisoner) Southwell sat and contemplated the man opposite in complete silence. So this was the creature who had terrified a city and killed one of its most innocent young women. This weedy, insignificant, pallid man of about thirty years of age. The pale eyes couldn't meet his own. The man looked everywhere except at Bob Southwell.

Bob might have sat in silence for an hour if the man had not burst out, 'I'm not talking with her in the room.'

He was looking, or rather not looking, at Jenny Wren.

'Why not?' asked Bob.

'You don't know, nobody knows. I've been trying to show them.'

'Show who what?'

'Show people what women are. Underneath they are all the same.' He looked at Jenny with extreme distaste.

'All the same in what way? I would have said they were all completely different.'

'Oh no,' said the prisoner argumentatively. 'They are all alike. They tempt men to do horrible things, to be jealous, to hate each other. Look at the Trojan wars. All those brave warriors killed and all because of a woman who couldn't be faithful to her husband.'

Bob felt surprised. This unsavoury individual talking about the Trojan wars? This vicious murderer? There was a short silence, then the man began again.

'Even when they are old, they are still all sex, all big—' he gestured at his chest—'all bum and tits. I'm not talking with her in the room and that's flat.'

'I should have thought most of us knew all that,' Bob remarked, and then said to Jenny, 'We'll get further with someone of the male gender. Sorry, Jenny. Get James.' To the tape recorder he said, 'DC Wren is leaving the room.'

Jenny didn't mind this sexual discrimination. She was glad to get away from that creep. James, who was trying to keep awake by drinking coffee and eating a sandwich in the canteen, looked surprised and pleased when he heard his instructions. He stood up, over-topping Jenny by about a foot, and crammed the last of his sandwich into his mouth.

'Haven't you stopped growing yet,

336

James?' said Jenny tartly, as though it was all his own fault. He grinned.

'My mother says I have got hollow legs.'

'And thin with it.'

Jenny gave him a playful punch in the ribs and he pretended to double up with pain, groaning.

'What's he like then?' he asked a moment later, picking up the ball-point pen and other bits and pieces he'd strewn around the table.

'Weird. Just your type.'

'I know he's weird. There was that doll,' and James shuddered.

'You had better get there. The boss wanted you pronto, not after you'd finished your sandwich. Go on, Carrot Top.'

'Carrot tops are green,' said James as he made for the canteen door.

'That's right, James,' Jenny called after him.

As James settled down in the interview room there was a definite change in the prisoner's attitude. So much so that Bob Southwell wondered if he had been right to give in. He might have got further more quickly if he had filled the room with policewomen, busty ones if available, and frightened the wits out of the prisoner.

'You're going to tell everyone?' the prisoner asked Bob Southwell almost eagerly. 'Will it be in all the papers?' He gave a little high giggle. That giggle sealed something about him in Southwell's mind. He's a nut case, he thought. Stark raving bonkers.

'I'm sure it will,' said a grim-faced Southwell.

'Then I will have succeeded, at least partly. And it won't matter what happens to me.'

'What do you think will happen to you?' Bob was curious.

'Prison, I suppose.' The man was vague. His very appearance was vague. It was not surprising that there had been so many different descriptions. He was of middle height, but might well have seemed gross and looming, a much bigger man, when striking down a woman.

'Let us begin at the beginning,' said

Bob Southwell. Who was running this interview, himself or the murderer? 'Your name is Saul South, you are thirty-three years old, born here in York ...'

'No, I wasn't,' said Saul South positively. 'I was born in Halifax, so they tell me. But seeing as my mother died when I was very young, they sent me to an auntie what lived in York, but she was married to a man from Middlesbrough who—'

'All right,' interrupted Southwell. 'You can tell all that stuff to the psychiatrists. I'm not concerned with your family history. Let's concentrate on those crimes you've been committing.'

'Oh, I haven't been committing any *crimes*,' said the prisoner. 'Not *crimes*. I've been on a crusade. I suppose it is over now. It will be difficult to crusade from prison. But if I am famous perhaps I might be able to. Write articles for the newspapers and that.'

'You have been attacking women. You murdered one poor girl.'

'I didn't mean to *hurt* them of course,' said the prisoner confidingly. After so many years of hardly speaking, he seemed unable to stop. 'Not *hurt* them. I'm sorry about that girl, but she has me to thank, she never had time to get like the rest of them, damned.'

'All right, you admit to perpetrating these attacks?'

'Oh yes.' The prisoner was trying out the word 'perpetrating' for size. They could see his lips moving as he silently mouthed the syllables.

'What was the point of this crusade?' asked Bob Southwell wearily.

He wished he'd put the interview off till later, until next week, or a year come Christmas, instead of thinking it would be easier to get at the truth right away, before the prisoner had time to think about it. Most of the staff involved with the capture of Saul South had been up all night. Used though they all were to night duty, eyelids were dropping. Warm comfortable beds at home were tugging at their memories. The most hardened police officers were having mental pictures of mugs of Horlicks.

'You don't see it yet?' The prisoner

leaned across the table towards Southwell and fixed him with a burning look. The usually dull and lifeless eyes were transformed.

James Jester, not being in eye contact, found himself yawning. Whatever justification this brute found for his actions, James would always associate him with a desecrated doll, picked up by a maiden lady of irreproachable family and pure life on a scrap of waste ground behind a factory outlet warehouse. This—this creature before them, this filthy creature— he even smelled as though he needed a bath—had been leading a crusade, had he, against the female of the species? Pull the other one. Filthy pervert, thought James, revelling for once in taking a classic mindless macho attitude. At that moment, fighting sleep, revolted by the prisoner, remembering the dead girl's pathetically innocent body, he could easily have lapsed into thoughts quite foreign to him, and let phrases such as 'kick his head in' or 'thump the hell out of him' run through his mind. Civilised James. So what sort of life would this pervert lead in prison?

'A crusade,' he was saying, his lips wet at the corners and flapping. 'They are all the same under their clothes. Mantraps. Snares of Satan. However old they are and look as though they aren't Jezebel and Eve, shapeless old bags, they are all the same, rip their clothes off and then everyone can see that they are all the same ...' He came to a sudden stop and the light died out of his eyes.

'All right, Sonny.' Southwell got up from his chair. 'That's only more of what you were saying earlier. We've heard enough of your drivel. James, get someone to put him in a cell. We deserve a break from this.'

When James Jester returned Bob Southwell was still standing by the table in the interview room.

'Drive you home, sir?' asked James.

'I was thinking, James, that this is the way the Yorkshire Ripper started. By disarranging the clothes and nothing more. He soon went on to other things. Scratching was the next step, as this bloke inflicted superficial cuts in the process of removing their clothing.' Bob sighed and straightened up. 'I expect you are as tired as I am.'

'Oh, no, I'm not, sir. Fresh as a daisy. I know you haven't got your own car here so we could use one of the firm's. Have you home in five minutes.'

The following morning Bob Southwell stumbled into work still bleary-eyed after only a few hours' sleep. He had barely settled at his desk before the phone rang.

'Hallam here,' said a cheerful voice Bob could hardly recognise as Bruno's.

'Morning, sir.'

'Angela's home, with me. She will need care during the next few days, I am applying for compassionate leave. You will have to act for me, Robert.'

'I will do my best, sir.'

'Can you arrange to come to my house—let's say tomorrow afternoon, about half-past two? We can rustle up a cup of tea. You should have a lot to tell me.'

'How is Angela?' Bob reflected that he didn't know the girl's surname. He'd heard it sometime, though, and was sure it wasn't Hallam.

'She's still asleep, I think. But she will second my invitation, I know.'

'Thank you, sir. I will look forward to it.'

Bob put the phone down with a puzzled expression. What exactly had happened? There had been a rapturous reunion, but how had father and daughter become separated in the first place? Well, he'd find out. Invited to afternoon tea at Hallam's home, when he had virtually arrested the man only hours earlier! Was he going to escape scot free from whatever mess he'd got himself into? If so, Bob felt, he was luckier than he deserved to be.

The strange thing was that all his antagonism had gone. He looked back on the way he had felt—so unlike himself—and wondered how it had come about. He now felt balanced, whole, DCI Robert Southwell as he really was, once more.

16

Promptly at half-past two DCI Southwell presented himself at the front door of Bruno Hallam's house on the Badger Hill estate, which lies between the university at Heslington and the Hull road. From the outside there was nothing unusual about the house.

Hallam had bought a newer semi than Bob's own, which was 1960 vintage. This one was more like 1985. The front garden was probably unchanged from the previous owners; it had a rectangle of grass surrounded by narrow borders. At this time of year the borders were empty of the usual bedding plants. In the whole front garden there were only three or four shrubs, haphazardly planted, at present without their leaves.

'Come in,' said Bruno Hallam opening the door into the hall.

Bob realised before passing over the threshold that the atmosphere inside was unusual and unexpected. He stepped in and stood hesitantly, eye to eye with Bruno.

'Look, sir,' he said, 'I want to apologise. I had suspicions about your behaviour which were completely out of order.'

'If you don't move, Robert, I can't shut the door,' said his boss.

Robert moved to one side.

'Too cold to keep it open,' remarked Bruno, shutting it firmly. 'Come in and sit down.'

Bob didn't feel like accepting hospitality until he had made some sort of restitution.

'On Tuesday night I just about had you arrested,' he said.

'Forget it, Robert.' Hallam clapped him on the shoulder. 'I don't blame you. You had reason. I want to explain my side of it, that's one purpose in asking you here like this. Before we go through—Angela is well enough to get up and see company, she is waiting for us in the sitting-room—let me give you some background. Come into the

346

dining-room for a minute.'

Before following Bruno, Bob took a glance round. He realised that the gleaming woodblock flooring ran throughout the ground floor of the house, and so did the plain white walls and matt white woodwork. The air was warm but not hot. There was not much furniture. The hall had only a small wooden brightly polished table, and on it stood the telephone and a statuette, a blobby sort of thing. Above was a group of small pictures, delicate line drawings of nothing in particular. There was a faint smell of furniture polish and also of something good cooking, spicy—perhaps caraway—with vegetables, and meat.

The dining-room had several pictures, colourful oil paintings. The dining-table was a sheet of glass, over an inch thick, with a mass of bubbles evenly spread through the glass, yet not regular or in any pattern. The support under the glass was a simple frame of stainless steel. The chairs, of stainless steel and bands of black leather, stood against the walls.

Bruno was talking, trying to tell him something.

'You have gathered that I was once married. Women have a hard time as police wives, you know only too well, I suppose, Robert. Shift work, long hours, unexpected overtime, friends and neighbours looking sideways when they find out what you do. My wife grew tired of it after several years and we separated. Not my wish, you understand.'

Bob made a sympathetic sound.

'We had one daughter. I would have liked more children.'

Bruno paused, remembering. Then, 'At first after the divorce I had proper access, but when my wife remarried she started to be difficult about it. In the end my daughter and I ceased to meet.'

'That must have been very distressing for you,' and Bob's voice showed his sympathy.

'Angela and I hadn't met since she was nine years old. Until last night.'

Bruno's voice suddenly caused him

difficulty and he had to stop speaking to clear his throat.

'I know I blew my top with you, the day you had little Susan in the office. Robert, you don't know what it is like to lose a child.' He looked away.

To lose a child! I don't know what it is like! thought Bob. A chill went through him. He hoped he never knew what it was like.

Hallam went on. 'But it's only now, when I've got my Angela back, that I can be rational about it. Seeing you with your fair-haired daughter hit me in the solar plexus with the reminder of what I had missed and was still missing. It could have been Angela standing there. At that age she was so much like your Susan is now. All those lost years of childhood and the teenage years, my little daughter ...' Bruno Hallam's face seemed to shake with emotion and he fell silent.

'If I'd known, sir ...' said Bob awkwardly.

'My name is Bruno, Robert.'

After a while he went on, 'My wife even changed our daughter's name. She is at the

349

university under another man's name, my wife's second husband's name. You see I say "my wife". I still think of her like that. I have not even thought of remarrying.'

'If only I'd known, Bruno,' Bob said. 'I would have felt the same in your place. About seeing Susan, I mean. Unexpectedly.'

'I felt too strongly about it to tell you why, does that make sense? I didn't lose sight of my daughter entirely. When she applied for York University I applied for the superintendent's job. By the time I took over, the sequence of attacks were well under way. Hence the jogging round the university, which can be dropped now, thank goodness. I was on guard—useless, as it turned out.'

Hallam then opened the connecting double doors and led the way into the long through room. The gleaming woodblock floor and pure white walls and paintwork ran through this space too. Bob had realised by now that the paintings on the walls of the house were originals and probably very special. He was also looking at the small pieces of sculpture with a perceptive eye. The furniture in here reminded him of the table in the hall—warm, friendly. He didn't know the name but realised that it was a distinctive style. Began with a B, he thought. Biedermeier? Austrian, or somewhere near there?

Angela was sitting by the patio window, doing something with her hands. As Bob came nearer he could see that it was embroidery. Remembering his wife's friend, Julia, he realised that he knew what to call it. After greeting the girl, he asked, 'Is that canvas-work, Angela?'

She flashed a smile up at him.

'Not many men would know that,' she said. 'Even women tend to call it tapestry.'

'But tapestry is woven, isn't it?'

'You are quite right.'

Bruno quietly vanished into the kitchen. Bob sat down and looked at Angela. She looked pale and ill, but not too bad considering what she had been through. Her smile had been a good one, not small or struggling.

'You don't look too bad after your

experience,' he said.

'I thought you would be telling me off, Mr Southwell.'

'When you are completely better I probably will.'

'I can't concentrate well enough to read or study, and Papa and I have talked ourselves out for the time being. This is very soothing,' she said, lifting her stitchery to show him what she meant. 'I can just about manage to do a bit.'

He could see that the little picture was of tree branches in front of a large moon.

'Nice,' he said.

Bruno came back in with a loaded tray, little sandwiches and cake as well as biscuits and tea. The refreshments looked delicious and the tea was thin and pale and fragrant. Bob settled down to enjoy himself. The tensions had gone. He looked at Bruno and felt not a trace, not the faintest whisper, of resentment. Instead he felt a sudden and unexpected warmth.

'Afternoon tea is so civilised,' remarked Bruno.

'Do you mind me remarking on your

home?' Bob asked. 'It has such an unusual atmosphere, very intriguing.'

Bruno looked at him in silence for a moment, then said, 'You don't know very much about me, do you, Bob?'

'Personally, no, I suppose not.'

'Why should any of us be interested in the ancestors of another member of the force? But in my case it is relevant, since the atmosphere intrigues you.'

Bruno sipped his tea and paused as though wondering how much to divulge. At last he said, 'My mother was from Vienna. Shortly before the beginning of the 1939–45 war she came over here as a child refugee. Her parents didn't make it. She was fostered, in Sheffield, and later went to art college. She was very poor, of course. At college she met my father, some years older than she, also Viennese.'

Bob Southwell wondered whether to say anything, but decided not to. He looked attentively at Bruno, who went on talking, slowly and thoughtfully, almost as if to himself.

353

'My father's family had been well-established international art dealers for some generations. They were particularly successful in the Edwardian era, friendly with King Edward VII himself. They had had a gallery in London and another in Vienna. So when Red Vienna stopped being Red when it was overrun by the Nazis, my father was fortunate enough to have a ready-made home in London. He got his parents away also. The London gallery had long since gone the way of all good things. The only family member still living in London by that time was my great-aunt, but she had kept on the old family home. They had been wealthy once, and the big house was her own. We were extremely fortunate, and were not alone in that. Members of what one might call the international set had been like the wise virgins. Not all refugees were poor.'

'You were brought up in London, then?' asked Bob Southwell.

'No! Certainly not. Perish the thought,' and Bruno smiled. 'No. Due to the bombing in London, my father and his parents went north to an old suburb of Sheffield; the city was later blitzed. My parents had found a house no one wanted at that time, too large. I was born in that house. Great-aunt had sent up a removal van full of family furniture, china, linen, paintings for us to use. The London house was so stuffed it was hard to move, she was happy to let us have some of the contents. Most of the paintings were those by young unknown artists the firm had been encouraging at one time or another, or painters and sculptors who had not become fashionable. That's the story of the art here.'

'Were your family still dealers?'

'No. I told you the London gallery had closed, long before. The relatives living in England had retired comfortably. We had to set about earning money for ourselves. My father had had an art training. As he could not be a dealer, he taught drawing at the Sheffield college where my mother was a student.'

'And you have the family possessions here,' said Bob.

'Eventually I inherited all of them. Some of those struggling young artists of many years ago have became famous. The drawings in the hall are by Klee, and the paintings in the other room by Kandinsky. Too valuable now to pay the insurance on them, so we just enjoy them.'

'And your furnishings are all family things?'

'A house is easier to look after if it is sparsely furnished. My family tended to stuff them full of objects. Most of it is in store at present. But you will understand why you found the atmosphere different, let us say.'

'Hallam is not an Austrian name, though, is it?' Bob ventured.

A few days before, he would not have believed that he would ever be enjoying delicious fairy-tale biscuits and fragrant weak tea in Bruno's sitting-room, let alone asking personal questions.

'It is my real name. You should know, Bob, that a surname is not as fixed a thing as is a forename—a Christian name. One can change a surname almost at will. The new one is as legitimate as the previous one.'

'It was the pictures that drew my attention most,' said Bob, determined to get off the subject of surnames and grandfathers. 'I like the ones by Klee.'

'Klee,' said Hallam, pronouncing it differently. 'A Swiss artist influenced by Dadaism, which was described by someone as "serious artistic buffoonery". Pretty accurate, don't you think so? He was also influenced by the Blue Rider group, particularly Macke.'

'Of course,' said Bob, who had never heard of any of these artists.

'Daddy!' said Angela. 'You are boring Mr Southwell with all this!'

'"Shut thee gob", you mean, do you, daughter?' said Bruno in a broad Sheffield accent, with a smile on his face.

Angela turned to Bob.

'I think the only thing to remember about Klee is that he called drawing "taking a line for a walk". Such a fun thing to think, don't you agree?'

'I see the point, having looked at his pictures,' he answered her with a pleased look. If art could be explained as simply as that even he might begin to understand it.

At that moment the front doorbell rang. Bruno went to answer it and came back almost immediately with an armful of flowers.

'For you, Angela,' he said, 'from one Tudor Evans and some of your other fellow students.'

'Pops!' said Angela reproachfully. 'You aren't supposed to read the messages.'

She took the flowers with a slightly self-conscious look, knowing that her father was watching her.

'Isn't it lovely of them? I had better put these in water,' she said, leaving the room.

'I never supposed I should have her to myself for long,' Bruno said to Bob.

'She must have many admirers,' sympathised Bob.

'And probably none of them will turn

out to be serious? I'm sure you are right. I would like her to marry someone I can respect and be on friendly terms with. But ...'

The two men were silent until Angela returned with the flowers in a container.

'Isn't it kind of Tudor and the others?' she said. 'There are so many I need more vases, Papa.'

Justice took its course.

The middle-aged man who had scrawled the graffiti on Jenny Wren's car was tried for all the offences that could be made to fit the crime.

Spendlove, the ex-con, the vagrant, went to ground.

Dr Blow's wife obtained a legal separation and supported their children by going back to her job as an archivist. He charmed one of the students into becoming his mistress, then began to systematically dominate her.

Saul South was awaiting trial for murder. The other charges lay on the book.

Life in the York police force had never been so tranquil. It was some weeks later that Bruno Hallam went into Bob Southwell's office with a paper in his hand.

After a morning greeting, he said, 'Have you seen this advert, Robert?'

And Bruno strolled to look out of the window while Bob Southwell read the paragraph marked with yellow.

'How should it interest me?' asked Bob.

'Think about it. I applied for this post at York because Angela was coming to the university, and I intend to stay at least until she finishes her degree course. Then I shall reconsider my situation. Now you want promotion to the detective superintendent grade. No chance here for two years unless I fall under a bus. There is a post going elsewhere, open competition, why not try for it?'

For a while Bob could not say anything.

'You mean for me to apply?'

'Only if it is what you want.'

There was another silence, broken by Bruno Hallam.

'You would have got York if I hadn't

put in for it, Robert. If you are interested in that job, it is my bet you will get it, particularly with a good recommendation from me.'

'That's good of you,' said Bob.

'Not at all.'

'I will show it to Linda. Bruddersford! It would mean leaving York and she does love the place.'

'You would not be so far away.'

'We will talk it over tonight.'

Angela had taken refuge from the winter weather in the History section of the Morrell Library. She had changed her preferred seat. The new computer building was going up fast and the view she had loved so much, of Siward's Howe and the water tower on top of the hill, had gone. All that was left was her memory of it and an embroidery in her drawer. So she had begun to favour the other side of the library.

She sat down just as a tall young man and a girl got up from their desks and walked out, hand in hand. On his face was a look of pride and on hers the slightly bemused expression of love. Her dark hair flowed over her shoulders. She was short, her head barely reaching his shoulder. She was curvaceous. She was Jessica. She walked out without noticing Angela.

So much for the Women's Group, and Angela smiled to herself. In a moment she could see their lives laid out before them. 'We met as students at York University,' they would tell their friends down the years. Those first sweet moments would come back to them from time to time when they caught each other's look and simultaneously remembered, his hand for the first time on hers, those first public affirmations which had ended in a semi-detached house full of nappies and babies and at last the detached house and the teenage children, and perhaps her return to some career or other. But, remembering her friend's face, the look of fulfilment glowing from the two of them, Angela wondered if the career would ever be started ...

Well, if she went across the bridge to the restaurant for her lunch, she would not need to eat alone. Tudor would be there with some of his friends. It was a comforting thought. Angela started work on her essay, 'Mrs Gaskell's view of women's role in society'.

The publishers hope that this book has given you enjoyable reading. Large Print Books are specially designed to be as easy to see and hold as possible. If you wish a complete list of our books, please ask at your local library or write directly to: Magna Large Print Books, Long Preston, North Yorkshire, BD23 4ND, England.

This Large Print Book for the Partially sighted, who cannot read normal print, is published under the auspices of

THE ULVERSCROFT FOUNDATION

THE ULVERSCROFT FOUNDATION

. . . we hope that you have enjoyed this Large Print Book. Please think for a moment about those people who have worse eyesight problems than you . . . and are unable to even read or enjoy Large Print, without great difficulty.

You can help them by sending a donation, large or small to:

**The Ulverscroft Foundation,
1, The Green, Bradgate Road,
Anstey, Leicestershire, LE7 7FU,
England.**

or request a copy of our brochure for more details.

The Foundation will use all your help to assist those people who are handicapped by various sight problems and need special attention.

Thank you very much for your help.